PRIDE,
PANCAKES, &
PARIS

By Emmie J. Holland

ISBN: 979-8-9863115-2-4
EDITOR: Kenna Karlsson
COVER ARTIST: initial by gemmarakia, edited by meghanly
PROOFREADING: Reanna Guthrie

To Becca (@thenightstandbook)
Because one time we talked about plants, and it resulted in this
entire book.

Trigger Warnings

Dear reader,

      It is my desire to ensure that everyone who picks up this book feels comfortable in doing so. Because of this, I have provided a list of trigger warnings.

      Car Accident
      Alcohol Use
      Underage Drinking
      Injured Family Member
      Explicit Sexual Scenes
      Swearing

ONE

Georgia

I am a murderer.

I mean, as far as murderers go, I'm actually pretty tame. At least the murder wasn't brutal and bloody. It was slow, executed over three months' time, and certainly accidental.

That is . . . probably worse.

I wince, holding the glass mason jar in my hand as I narrow my eyes. I sincerely hope the dry and crumbling parade roses can feel my judgment. It was kind of rude to go and die on me.

Granted, I didn't water them the way I should have. My grip tightens on the cool class as the wilted flowers mock me. It's *definitely* my fault, but the drooping flowers are a good metaphor for my life, anyway.

I'm either spending too much time in the classroom trying to piece together this entire student-teacher gig, or I'm home, watching *Netflix*, eating copious amounts of kettle corn, and avoiding doing literally anything for as long as humanly possible.

It's a delicate balance between too much and too little.

No wonder my soul is dead.

Like the plant.

I dump the rest of the water into the dirt and hope it does something. It is entirely possible that I've discovered the fountain of youth here in my apartment, and my poor plant child will magically be cured in a matter of moments. Besides, drinking more water is the cure for most things. Constipated? Drink water. Acne? Drink water. Slowly dying because your student teaching placement is in a high school, and your students think you're so pitiful that they put together a GoFundMe to help you replace your *stupid* shoes? Grab that emotional support water bottle, and—you guessed it—drink water.

I look back at the plant, now drenched and still very much dead. "You'll be just fine," I mutter.

The door bursts open, startling me as I spin to see my roommate, Emerson, plow into the room. Grocery bags filled with pipe cleaners, dried macaroni noodles, and other miscellaneous craft supplies spill onto the couch like she's just in the beginnings of her brand-new hoarding disorder. When her brown eyes hit me, I can already tell she has come with bad news. Hopefully, it has little to do with hoarding. "Don't kill me."

I look back at the plant—my first victim. "Sorry, I was actually just practicing." A smile tugs at the corner of my mouth.

Emerson untangles her beige backpack strap from her long, black hair, looking at my crime scene. "Right," she says. "So, anyway." She's dragging her words out like she knows I will *not* be okay with whatever comes next.

Emerson and I have roomed together since freshman year. I've spent holidays with her family, and she's spent holidays with mine. After four years of solid friendship, I can typically tell when she's about to say something I won't like, and this is one of those moments.

"Spit it out," I say.

"You know how much I love my job performing at the bar, right? It's almost as much as I love having you there. Which you're going to be—there, I mean."

"Of course." I chuckle, folding my arms across my chest and waiting for her to continue.

"Sawyer is going to be there, too."

I blink—loudly. If you can even do that.

Silence stretches between us as I stare at her and wait for the punch line, but it doesn't come. I swear I hear a car swerve outside, birds dropping dead, babies crying, a sinkhole forming in the street.

"When you say Sawyer," I question.

"Yes." Her smile isn't exactly happy. Her teeth are showing, but she kind of looks like she's cringing. "My brother."

I literally don't respond. If there is one thing more abusive than a classroom full of high school students learning about Environmental Science, it's Sawyer Owens.

I first met Emerson's family during Thanksgiving, our freshman year. Since Emerson's family lives locally, and my family lives halfway across the country, I skipped paying for a second ticket when I would be home at Christmas, anyway. The Owens family is made of some of the nicest people on the planet—minus one—and when I mentioned I was in school to study secondary education, Sawyer chimed in.

I don't know if it was the, *you realize education is a shitshow right now,* or the, *well, those who can't, teach.* Whatever it was, somewhere between his infuriatingly handsome smile and his stunningly poor social awareness, I made my decision.

I hate him.

No. Scratch that. I *loathe* him.

And he has confirmed those feelings every single day since the moment I met him.

Now he's some hot sous chef at one of the restaurants in town, and something about that infuriates me even more.

Emerson walks forward, her eyes pleading in a way that reminds me I cannot say no. I've skipped out on watching her perform too many times since student teaching started. I can't do it again. She loves this job. She's proud of it. I can't *not* go.

She places her hands on my shoulders. "Oh, come on, Georgia! It'll be fun."

I scoff. "I may just stay home."

"Look," Emerson glances behind me, smirking when she sees my withering roses. "I know you feel bad about the plant, but he isn't coming back. You don't need to stay home because he is long gone."

I keep my face blank, my tone dry. I am obviously going to be spending my Friday night torturing myself by hanging out with her brother, but she doesn't need to know that yet.

"Jesus rose from the dead," I say.

She tries not to laugh, nodding her head to all the death behind me. "*That* is not Jesus."

"Jesus also raised *other* people from the dead." I blink again, keeping my features schooled even though I'm dying to laugh at her confused expression. "Your mom's a Catholic," I add. "She gets it."

"You said you'd be at this show, so we could hang out afterward." Her hands fall away from my shoulders. "You're practically working a full-time job now, *and* you're working on your final project." She's not convinced. "I know you'd never miss an opportunity to hang out with the one, the only—"

She's gesturing to herself. Her megawatt smile would put a car salesman to shame.

"Stop while you're ahead." My smile cracks the façade, and I laugh. "Fine," I say, but she already knew that was the answer. "But one, I am not straightening my hair for this."

She practically skips to the couch to gather up whatever craft supplies she purchased. "I don't know why you'd disrespect your curls like that, anyway."

I glance down at the blonde rat's nest hanging below my shoulders and shrug. When I look at her again, her arms are full, and she's slowly making her way toward the hallway and to her room.

"And two," I say. "If he says *one* thing about my clothes, or my major, or anything negative whatsoever—"

"Yeah, yeah," she shouts, and I hear her kicking her door open. "If he comments on your outfit, you can come back and play Easter with your sad excuse for a plant."

I chuckle, making my way to the kitchen so I can finally eat something. During my lunch, I usually scarf down fruit snacks and pretzels because twenty minutes is never enough, especially when five of those minutes are used up peeing for the first time all day. I pull out the bread, peanut butter, and jelly, setting them on the counter and crafting a dinner of champions.

"Sous chef," I mutter. "I hope he'd take one look at this meal and be horrified."

TWO

Georgia

I had to change before we headed out to The Outpost where Emerson performs on the weekends. If you've ever worked in education, then you understand that no matter the age group, you always come home feeling like you're covered in germs and boogers.

Teaching has slowly become my entire life—my entire personality.

My entire wardrobe.

My only saving grace is that The Outpost is a smaller bar, and I don't think anyone will notice that I'm wearing a black science t-shirt that says *you matter* next to a bubbling beaker and some overalls that definitely cover the words.

It's fine.

It's better than being in bed by eight, which happens to be in thirty minutes. At least I'm out.

"You could walk a little faster!"

I smile, following Emerson down the busy sidewalk. It isn't dark yet, but by the time we leave, I will be able to check *nocturnal partier* off my bucket list. "Sorry," I say, catching up to her quickly. "You could be a bit nicer. I am mourning a very important loss right now."

She gives me an exasperated look. "Don't worry, Jesus, you'll have your friend alive and breathing in no time."

I laugh as she drags me closer to the bar. The wooden sign sticks out from the brick building on the strip and highlights our destination—Emerson's pride and joy. The sign used to hang crooked, but someone decided that was probably bad for business and fixed it.

I can't say I don't agree.

"Hey!" Emerson bursts forward, releasing my hand and wrapping her arms around a much taller, brown-haired, athletically built, perfectly and infuriatingly created, Sawyer.

If I had any ounce of joy on my face before, it's gone now.

"Sorry we're late," she continues, pulling back from his embrace. Something about the thought of being embraced by a literal asshole has me wanting to vomit. It would be much nicer if his face looked like an actual rectum. Maybe his insults wouldn't hurt so badly.

I chuckle at my own thoughts as Emerson continues. "Georgia was trying to resurrect a dead plant, and you know how that goes."

"Shouldn't an Environmental Science teacher be able to keep a plant alive?" His deep voice grates on me, and when his brown eyes turn to look at me, I instantly want to punch him in the face.

It's been less than a minute.

Good thing Emerson can be very forgiving.

This is going to be fun.

Sawyer's eyes rake down my body, taking in the gray canvas slip-on sneakers, my denim overalls, and my t-shirt he obviously can't read.

A pity, really. Since it's hilarious.

When the smile cracks across his face, he folds tan arms over his well-built chest. I want to gag. "You know." I roll my eyes prematurely, but he doesn't take the hint. "Wearing farmer-style overalls won't fix your plant. You can't aesthetic your way into having a green thumb."

Okay, *rude.*

I deadpan. "We're leaving."

Emerson grabs my arm, and I'm pretty sure all five-foot-two of her could break it and leave me bleeding on this sidewalk.

"She's joking," Emerson says, offering a wide smile to her brother.

I look back at him and his *plain* black t-shirt. How boring. "She's really not," I say. While I am *not* joking, I'm definitely not leaving. For one, this means too much to Emerson, and for two, if I can survive sixteen-year-olds bullying me all day and still want to teach, one night with this man won't break me.

I think Emerson might be doubting my commitment, though, since she's glaring at me. Nope. No, she just wants me to behave.

Gladly.

I offer Sawyer an even wider smile, one that makes

his smile look amateurish. "I'll stay," I say, tilting my head to the side and daring him to say something else.

He raises a brow at me. "Great."

"Great."

"Anyway!" Emerson chimes in. You guys will have time to eat during my sound check, but if I want something for dinner, we better go in now."

"Lovely," I say, with too much enthusiasm.

Sawyer and I are locked in the staring contest of the century. I'm just waiting for the next dig, the next thing that will have me imagining my hands around his throat and squeezing—hard.

God, I really am a murderer.

Jesus, forgive me.

"Fantastic," Sawyer says, satisfied. "I'm starved."

"I'm not," I say, offering a smug smile. Pushing past him, I open the glass door at the bar's entrance and toss my next statement over my shoulder. "I already had a PB and J."

The bar is mostly empty, but that won't last long. Emerson is good, *really* good. I spent our entire freshman year listening to her play her keyboard and sing her little heart out. Most roommates would be annoyed, but I liked it. It filled our shitty dorm room with life—joy. And now that she gets to play on stage every Friday and Saturday, I get to see that same joy over and over.

Well, not a lot recently, but that's why I'm not leaving.

I hear shoes tapping the wooden floor behind me, and then I feel someone grip my arm. I whirl, horrified to see Sawyer smiling down at me. He looks like a feral cat, ready to attack any second.

"A PB and J?" he asks, and it almost sounds like he's making fun of me. The touch from his hand still wrapped around my bicep literally burns. It's scalding hot—like the fiery pits of hell. "Really, Georgia," he continues, refusing to remove his torture grip. "I can make you something better than that."

"Unnecessary," I say, shrugging out of his hold and shaking off my disgust. I look up at him, smiling again because I know how to play nice. "You may be some fancy sous chef, or whatever, but I happened to enjoy my dinner."

"Did it highlight the very peak of your cooking talents?" His tongue rolls along his cheek, brown eyes lighted with amusement.

I smile wider. "Well, you know what they say," I begin, my tone dripping poison. "Those who can't—"

"Teach," he finishes with me.

He's still smiling and standing far too close as he towers over me. Whatever height genetics Emerson inherited; Sawyer did not inherit the same. I'm five-seven, and he still dwarfs me. I do, however, like to think he still lies on whatever dating app he uses. He's probably six-two. I hope he says six-four, and his lies lead to girls walking out on every first date. I hope he's lonely—miserable even.

"You remembered," he says, almost flattered.

"How could I forget?" I respond. My eyes flick to Emerson, who is talking to the owner closer to the entrance. She nods our way as if she's informing him about us, probably explaining that we are with her and not to kick us out. How unfortunate.

Looking back at Sawyer, I finish my statement. "Especially since you weren't the one to invent the saying. Rude *and* unoriginal."

He huffs a stale laugh before Emerson is in front of us again.

"I have fifteen minutes to eat, and then we are doing the sound check," she says. "I got a wrap since it'll be out faster. You guys, however, can order whatever you want."

Emerson grabs my hand and drags me over to the booth in the corner, Sawyer following at our heels. I can tell she's excited, and it's nice to see her so passionate about something. I smile, trying to soak in her positivity and willing it to take away any murderous thoughts that may have leaked into my mind.

It wouldn't be kind to kill her brother at her show. That would make me a terrible friend, and I am not about to be a terrible friend.

I glance back at Sawyer, tossing him a genuine smile—one that says, your sister deserves all the happiness in the world.

When we sit down, I order an avocado bacon club and a side of sweet potato fries. And despite my unwillingness to admit defeat, I have to say that in the back of my mind; I know the truth about the sandwich. It is sure as shit way better than the sad toddler meal I made for myself earlier.

THREE

Sawyer

The first time Emerson introduced me to her college roommate, I had been pleasantly surprised.

Georgia showed up to our family Thanksgiving with her curly blonde hair piled on top of her head, an oversized sweater dress, and a store-bought pack of those artificial sugar cookies with orange icing and brown sprinkles.

Or was it brown icing and orange sprinkles?

Doesn't matter. When I first saw her standing there, I thought I was going to have a really hard time *not* hitting on Emerson's new friend. Something my sister instructed firmly against in the days prior.

But then Georgia opened her mouth.

I smiled at the cookies, walked them into the kitchen, and said, "You can put them next to the ones I made. Just set yours on the end of the island by the trash."

I can admit that I didn't phrase it right.

In my defense, the trashcan was at one end of the island. I wasn't telling her to throw them away.

Her hazel eyes hardened, and her mouth hung open. I could see the wheels turning, the way she zeros in on her prey.

"Emerson said you were *trying* to become a chef." She held up one of the cookies I made, iced to look like a cartoon turkey. She took one bite, opened the trash, and dumped it while saying, "Don't quit your day job. If my store-bought cookies belong in the trash, then yours do too." She scoffed, muttering *chef* on the way out of the kitchen, and when she exited into the living room, she charmed the pants off my parents.

Arrogant.

Rude.

Condescending.

Staring at me.

"What?" I say, looking at her from across the table of our booth. Emerson is already on the stage up front as guests fill in. It's been a while since I've watched her play, but my sister has real talent. When she asked me to come, how could I say no? I couldn't. Georgia or no Georgia.

"I asked you how playing high-ranking chef is going. Has the restaurant fired you for your attitude yet?" Georgia pops half of a sweet-potato fry into her mouth. I hate her mouth. It is both gorgeous and vile at the same time.

"They haven't fired me for my attitude," I respond, pulling my glass of water to my lips. "A simple, *how is your job going?* would have sufficed. I think you're spending too much time with children."

She scowls at me, turning to watch the stage. The bar has filled substantially, and Emerson has disappeared, probably getting a drink of water before her time to shine.

She's always been like this—talented. Even when she was belting out songs from Broadway in high school. I used to get on her about singing while I was playing video games. Literally, all of my buddies could hear her in the background while we were getting ambushed.

I definitely yelled at her, but when I left for school, I missed hearing her music. I wouldn't tell her that now—or maybe I would. What does it matter? I mean, look at her.

Emerson stands on the stage, gripping the microphone and introducing herself. When my eyes slide to Georgia, she is glowing, too. The one positive thing I can say about her is that she's been a good friend to my sister. At the very least, she's done that.

When Emerson sings, the entire bar goes wild, and nothing can rip the smile from my face. I'm just so fucking proud of her.

"Do you want a beer?"

"What?" I turn back to Georgia, shouting because, between the crowd and the loud music, it's difficult to hear. Also, if she said what I think she said, I'm pretty sure hell has frozen over.

"I asked if you wanted a beer," the ice queen says.

Hell has definitely become a hockey rink.

I stare at her, my brows furrowing. "Oh," I clear my throat. "Sure. Do you want me to Venmo you?"

"No, Mr. Sous Chef. You don't have to Venmo me. I'll just pay for it out of the money I make selling fancy worksheets online."

I can't tell if she's being sarcastic. "Like teacher worksheets?"

She rolls her eyes. "Yes, teacher worksheets." Scooting out of the booth, Georgia strides to the bar.

"Don't worry, I'll Venmo you."

I pull out my phone, reading a text message from Warren.

Warren: You and your girl have your passports, right? Sadie wants to make sure everything is ready since the wedding is in just over a week. You know how it is.

What girl? I want to say, but I just can't bring myself to admit that Anna dumped me.

Warren has been my friend since high school, and he is getting married in two weeks. His soon-to-be wife, Sadie, is incredibly nice, and her parents are extremely well off. Thus, the Paris wedding. I'm thankful to be going since I haven't seen Warren in over a year, but the fact that my girlfriend dumped me before he even got to meet her—

I don't want to touch the situation with a ten-foot pole. I shift uncomfortably and shove any and all feeling into the fiery furnace of *ignoring*.

It's been three weeks, and I still haven't told Warren. Which is really shitty of me because they are paying for the hotel, the meals, the plus one.

I just thought maybe once she had some time alone. No, nope.

Me: Yeah, it's all good to go.

I open up the app to pay Georgia. I'm not sure how much the drink is going to cost, so I round up to fifteen. Emerson told me she's student teaching, and when you're student teaching, you practically hold a full-time teaching position while attending the occasional night class and working on a final project. That and licensure exams. The girl doesn't have money. She shouldn't be buying anyone anything.

To save myself from appearing too kind, I type out the reasoning for my payment, knowing full well anyone on Venmo can see it.

Feet Pics ;)

I laugh, leaning back and shoving my phone back into my jean pocket.

"Here you go." Georgia places a bottle in front of me, finding her spot at the other side of the table, and we watch Emerson finish out her set.

In the middle of what I assume to be her last song, Georgia finally takes out her phone. I try to hide my smile by bringing my beer to my lips. Her infuriated expression tells me I struck the right nerve.

"You're fucking kidding, Sawyer."

I'm trying so hard not to laugh. Her eyes are as wild as her hair.

"My *mom* is friends with me on Venmo! She's going to think I'm selling pictures of my feet to strange men on the internet." She's shoving her phone screen in my face, displaying proof of my fifteen-dollar payment and the comment on it.

"Come on, my name is right there. I'm sure your mom knows about me. You probably talk about me all the time; she'll know it's a joke." I lean back in the booth, staring at her. She looks like a bomb about to go off, and something about that brings me a gross amount of satisfaction.

Her eyes are more vibrant when she's angry. Greener.

"You know, your eyes kind of look like lake water. Has anyone ever told you that before?"

She grunts—or shrieks. I can't really tell. She practically throws her phone down on the table. "And you are an arrogant, selfish asshole. Has anyone ever told *you* that before? Or are you too busy parading around with women who fawn over you just because you can cook a few measly meals?"

Ouch. . .

I try to hide my wince because actual *ouch*. That wound is still too fresh. Anna and I were together for seven months before she dumped me, and I haven't had a single woman fawn over me because I'm a chef. I'd like to think it's my charming personality.

Anna decided the personality wasn't enough.

"That was a low blow," I say. Frustration is quickly replacing the sting of her words, and I grip the bottle tighter.

"And I would do it again in a heartbeat."

"What's going on?" Emerson is walking up to the table, sliding in next to Georgia on her side of the booth.

Georgia gives a satisfied smirk, like she knows my sister is already taking her side.

Just because she didn't sit next to me doesn't mean that blood isn't thicker than water.

"Nothing," Georgia says, plastering on a fake smile. We both know how important this job is to Emerson, and I'm sure she doesn't want to ruin her night, just like I don't.

When Emerson looks away to wave at some of the other guests, I mouth the word *liar* to Satan sitting across the booth.

She practically snorts.

"So, Sawyer," Emerson starts. "Are you excited about Paris? I wish I could spend my spring break eating baguettes and drinking French coffee."

I grunt, keeping my hands around my beer bottle because I'm afraid if I let go, my face will give it away. Emerson knows Anna and I broke up. I called her the day after it happened, asking for advice, which she gladly gave.

"As ready as I'll ever be. You could come," I say. "I have an extra ticket now." I offer her a wan smile.

"What happened?" Georgia chimes in. "One of your adoring fans find out your brownies were actually from the box?"

Emerson looks concerned as she turns to Georgia. Her pained expression looks too much like pity for my comfort. Her eyes flick to me once before she reveals my secrets.

"Anna broke up with him," she says.

"Oh shit."

"Oh shit," I say, taking another drink of beer.

"Warren doesn't know." I'm talking to Emerson now. "He still thinks I'm bringing a date. I guess I thought maybe," I pause, looking at Georgia once before continuing. "I thought maybe she'd change her mind. You could use the ticket. I'm sure it wouldn't be difficult to change the name on it. It's also during your spring break."

"I can't," Emerson says. "I took extra nights here at the bar. Graduation is sooner than we think, and I still haven't secured a job." She looks uncomfortable. "I haven't been looking too hard. I like performing here, and to be honest, I'm not sure why I got the marketing degree. Maybe to satisfy Mom and Dad."

"You know they wouldn't have cared." It's true. Our parents would have supported Emerson in whatever she wanted. She's usually the one putting pressure on herself.

She sits up abruptly, eyes whipping between me and her roommate.

"Take Georgia!" she says.

"What, no!" For the first time in the history of the universe, Georgia Clark and I are in unison.

"No, listen," Emerson starts. "Georgia couldn't get a ticket to go back to her parent's place in Portland. I'm working all week. She'd be alone, anyway."

"I can't afford a trip to Paris!" Georgia screeches.

"Technically, the trip is paid for." I take another swig of my beer, trying to wash the bile back down my throat. The thought of spending an entire ten days in France with Georgia is utterly ridiculous.

"You have your passport." Emerson faces Georgia, talking as if this is the best idea she's ever come up with.

It's not.

But I'm not going to say that out loud.

"There's only one hotel room for me and my guest," I chime in, hoping it will deter her.

"Hotel rooms always have pull-outs or whatever. It's not even a big deal. It's ten days in *Paris*."

I'm staring at my sister. I'm not sure why she thinks this is such a great idea. The ticket is non-refundable, and I'm sure I can find someone else before then.

My phone vibrates in my pocket, and I pull it out to see a text message from Warren.

Warren: Sadie and I are really excited to meet her, bro.

My stomach twists painfully. He's getting *married*. What kind of friend would I be if I showed up at his destination wedding with all of my relationship problems?

I'm staring at Georgia, who looks like she's about to vomit, while Emerson goes on and on about how deserving she is of a break—a vacation.

It hits me all at once. I don't have to tell Warren at all. At least, not until after the wedding. He can have his day. I don't have to deal with my sorrow. It could work.

"Maybe you should come." The words are out before I can take them back.

Emerson and Georgia are looking at me now. Emerson's eyes are lighted with joy, Georgia's are . . . not.

My brow furrows.

"You're . . ." Georgia is speaking slowly now. "Excuse me. You're asking me to come with you?" The look of confusion on her face is almost cute—if she wasn't so awful. "To Paris."

I shrug. "Sure. We can both enjoy a trip. Stay away from each other while we're there. I'll even let you sleep on the pull-out couch. I hear they're really nice in France."

She rolls her eyes.

Wait until she hears the rest of this ridiculous plan. I can't tell her that part yet. I'll save it for later. Maybe she'll be so excited about a trip to Paris, France, she won't mind pretending to be my girlfriend at the wedding.

Georgia's caring. She doesn't care for me, and she likes to pretend that she isn't, but she'll understand how my situation could ruin someone's big day. She'll play along for Emerson.

"I—" She can hardly speak, hazel eyes whipping between me and my sister.

"It's a tentative yes," Emerson says. "Georgia will go to Paris with you."

My sister drags her friend out of the booth, moving to the bar for what I assume can only be more drinks.

I sit on my ass, plastering a smile on my face. If I'm going to convince her to come, I better start working now.

Georgia keeps looking back at me as if she's waiting for me to reveal it was a prank all along.

I pull out my phone, typing out a message I may soon regret for the rest of my adult life.

Me: She can't wait to meet you guys, too.

FOUR

Georgia

Seven-fifteen is way too early for life to exist on the planet. In fact, I may already be dead.

I roll my window down and listen to the intercom in the Starbucks drive-thru. When the barista finally hits me with the, *what can I get for you* line, I think I fall in love with him. Only because it's seven-fifteen on a Monday morning, I'm about to enter the soul-sucking presence of sixteen-year-olds, and I'm pretty sure this barista is about to give me caffeine.

"Can I get a venti, iced, vanilla latte with two pumps of peppermint?"

I can already feel the high of my sugar and caffeine cocktail.

I love it.

"Sure. Can I get you anything else?"

A trip to Paris without *Sawyer Owens.* I don't say that

out loud, obviously. But ever since Friday night, I have been back and forth, and back again as it pertains to the trip. Emerson is right in some ways.

For one, I am currently in Michigan, and my parents live in Portland, Oregon. Since I'm student teaching, I can't afford to buy a ticket home for every break. I know I'm pretty good at creating lessons and worksheets that I can sell on the teacher resource website I found, but it doesn't do much beyond giving me Starbucks money. The money I'm currently using.

"No, that's all!" I say before getting the total for my overpriced drink and a kind promise that the barista will see me at the window.

Emerson sat across from me in our living room and explained exactly what was paid for already. My ticket would be covered, my hotel, breakfast that comes with my luxurious stay—

It's all sounding too good to be true.

I wince. The only downside is I would be staying with Sawyer. Emerson is convinced that since we hate each other equally, we will both be eager to get out of the other's presence and won't see each other at all.

The trip is almost free. I have enough to cover some food if I'm careful about my spending, and I'm sure there's plenty to do there.

My tentative yes is becoming an abso-fucking-lutly pretty fast.

I grab my drink and drive the rest of the way to the high school, parking in the student parking lot because I'm not technically staff. Even though I'm providing them with tons of free labor.

I even have to buzz in because students haven't arrived yet, and of course, I don't get a key.

Student teaching really is a scam. A good scam, because the experience is necessary. They throw you into the world of education and have you try out your sea legs for a bit. I can see how that is going to help in the future. The only issue I have is that I'm paying a college to work at a public school.

My bank account is literally crying.

Turning down the hallway, I wave to the secretary and watch the white and navy tiles that pass under my feet. When I get to the science classroom, my supervising teacher, Mrs. King, is already organizing the papers I dropped off yesterday.

I work with her on what grades to take, how much assignments will be worth, and she has to input them into the gradebook.

Again, I'm a teacher—but not quite.

"You entered those fast. Did you even get a full weekend?" I ask, setting my schoolbag on the counter at the front.

I really lucked out with Lindsay King. She's an experienced teacher, the kindest soul on the planet, the hardest worker, and she really cares about all her students. I've heard horror stories from my classmates about their supervising teachers.

Luckily, I won the lottery.

She chuckles, putting the last paper into the final student's mailbox. "I got more of a weekend since you're grading the papers and writing the lesson plans."

I smile, leaning against the countertop and drinking a sip of my latte. "You haven't checked my lesson plans in weeks."

She winks at me. "Because you're doing fine." Mrs. King walks to the back of the room, where she keeps the paperwork she fills out while observing me. So far, she hasn't said anything terrible—just helpful suggestions.

"Besides," she continues, "I'm getting old. This is like an early taste of retirement."

I laugh before turning to write the learning goal on the board, settling into the comfortable silence before popping to the center of the whiteboard to write *Diversity Means Stability.*

My classes have been learning about the benefits of diverse gene pools and their ecological value. I'm hoping to set up a debate over the good, the bad, and the ugly sides of GMOs. It ticks all the right boxes on my evaluation forms, and teenagers like to have angsty arguments anyway—I might as well make it educational.

A knock sounds at the classroom door, and I glance at my watch to check the time. It's only eight, which means I have fifteen minutes before my first class starts. Since students are just arriving, it's probably another teacher here to talk to Lindsay.

"Georgia."

My entire body goes rigid. My grasp on the dry-erase marker would put the incredible hulk to shame.

I whip my head around to see, you guessed it, Sawyer fucking Owens standing in my classroom.

"What are you doing here?" I ask, setting the marker in the tray at the base of the whiteboard. "How did you even know to come here?"

"Emerson, obviously." He seems irritated.

My eyes flick to my latte, and I re-evaluate my earlier theory about how much caffeine can actually help brighten my mood.

I stare at him.

He stares at me.

I think about holding him under water until the bubbles stop.

No wonder my plant died.

"Okay," I start. "Why are you here?" I look at my watch again. Three minutes after eight. Sawyer better make it quick, and then he better haul ass before my students get here.

One other detail about sixteen-year-olds; if you don't have a love-life, they will try to write the narrative for you. It doesn't matter who you talk to, they will carefully craft a cute couple's name, and single-handedly design your wedding invitations.

I cannot have them see me with Sawyer.

The last time they did this, it was with Rick, the school custodian.

Rick is in his seventies.

"I needed to get your answer about the trip." He shifts uncomfortably. "The real one."

Right.

"Couldn't you have just texted me like a normal human being?" My voice is leaking venom at this point. "Or are your precious chef hands too fragile for texting?"

He scoffs, folding his arms across his broad chest. He's wearing a maroon t-shirt and jeans.

I look down at my *It's like magic, but real,* t-shirt with the giant atom on the front, my black high-waisted jeans, and my white converse. My shirt is the same color as his again.

I want to kill another plant.

"Right," he says, stepping forward, and I step back a little. "So, the spot is still open. I know Emerson explained the details of what is and isn't paid for. I need to know if you're coming or not."

I look around the classroom and spot the giant bulletin board I put together on the far wall, the stack of papers on the counter that I haven't gotten to yet, the half-finished *Scientist of the Week* board I created, and the cabinet beneath the lab table that has an extra pair of shoes I left here a few weeks ago.

I practically live in this classroom.

I need a break.

"I've thought about it," I say carefully, turning my eyes back to him. I'm trying to figure out why he's offering to begin with. There has to be some sort of angle. He can't be offering me a free trip for no reason, but I really, really want to go. "I'd like France, I think."

His lip pulls up at one corner, and I give him a look of disgust. Is he . . . *happy?*

"Great. I'll get your number from Emerson and give you the rest of the details. There is a catch."

I fucking knew it.

I sigh, folding my arms. "Okay," I say. "Let me have

it."

"You'll have to go to the wedding with me." He winces.

Honestly, I kind of figured I wouldn't be able to hitch a ride to France for a destination wedding and *not* attend the wedding. It's still an incredibly good deal.

"That's fine," I offer.

Sawyer's eyes flick to Lindsay, who is now eavesdropping from the corner. He steps closer, lowering his voice. "You're going to have to pretend to be my date."

"What?" I'm screeching. I know I'm screeching, and when I look down at my watch and read eight-ten, I know at least half of the high school heard me. I'm surprised a student hasn't popped their head in to see what animal died.

"Stop being so dramatic." Sawyer rolls his eyes. "I can't tell Warren that I brought my sister's roommate so she could have a free trip to France. You're going to have to pretend to be my girlfriend for the night."

"*Girlfriend?*" That escalated quickly. It's one thing to be someone's date, it's another thing to be their girlfriend. "You want to lie to your best friend and tell them I'm your *girlfriend?*" It takes everything in me not to vomit when I say the last word.

Sawyer looks really uncomfortable now. I think this is the first time I've ever seen him nervous. He's rubbing the back of his neck, the sleeve of his t-shirt stretched tight around his bicep. His cheeks are pink.

Oh. My. God.

Pigs are flying over the roof right at this moment.

"Wait. Stop. Pause." I hold my hand up to prove my

point. "Are you—" I point at him and take one big step away. "No."

His eyes are wild, and suddenly he's acting confused. Oh, he's going to gaslight me when I call him out for sure.

I almost whisper, praying to the good lord that Lindsay can't hear me. I pray so hard that I'm certain Emerson's mom would be proud and buy me a rosary for my efforts. "Are you *actually* asking me out?"

"Oh my god." He's pinching the bridge of his nose, and for a moment, I'm certain he's going to gaslight me and tell me he isn't, but then I see he looks about as disgusted at the idea as I feel. "No, Georgia." His brown eyes meet mine, and he's dead-ass serious. "No."

"Then why are you asking me to pretend to be your *girlfriend?*" I see a red-headed student peek around the corner and run back out into the hallway. The nerves hit me instantly. I have to get him out of here. I look at my watch—eight-thirteen.

"It's a long story. Anna broke up with me. Warren's big day. I don't want to ruin it. Just—*fuck*."

"You can't say that here."

He looks exasperated. "In a *high school?* Georgia, you'd have to be an idiot to think these kids—you know what, never mind." He taps a finger on the counter at the front of the room. "I don't want to ruin his day. It's *one* night. Would it kill you to do someone a favor?"

For him? Yes. Yes, it would.

The need to get him out of this classroom intensifies, and deep down, I know where this is going. I don't want to spend my entire spring break alone in my college apartment.

I need a break, and I don't have the money to take one on my own.

Georgia. His girlfriend. You'd be pretending to be his girlfriend.

I turn the thought over in my mind and smile broadly up at him as it dawns on me. "You'd have to be nice to me for an entire evening. You wouldn't even be allowed to insult my outfit or tell me my eyes look like seaweed."

He looks confused, but I continue anyway—partially because I know what my answer is going to be, and partially because he has got to get out of my damn classroom in the next thirty seconds. I place my hands on his back and start shoving him toward the door.

"I'll go. It's fine. I'll play your little pretend game, but for now, *you* have to go."

When we get to the exit, he turns, and I swear I see something like relief in his eyes.

If that part didn't surprise me, the next thing he does, did.

Sawyer Owens, the biggest asshole on the planet, turns around and plants a kiss on my cheek.

I'm too stunned to speak.

"Thanks, Georgia."

And just like that, Sawyer leaves the classroom with the bell ringing upon his exit.

Miles, one of my students, is standing at the door with the most terrifying look on his face. He looks like he found the juiciest piece of gossip, and he's about to sell it to a tabloid for a fortune.

"Um." I'm being awkward. I know I am. "Good

morning, Miles. Have a seat.”

Miles throws his backpack on the ground and won't stop staring at me as the rest of my first-period pile into the classroom.

No. *No.*

Somehow, I make it to the start of class without Miles mentioning anything.

Lindsay is at the back of the room and ready to fill out whatever form she's required to do for today. I'm flustered as I make my way to the front to flick on the projector. Any minute now, that child is going to say something, and my life will be over.

Still, I really, *really* want to go to Paris, and I suppose *one* night of pretending to be Sawyer's girlfriend can't be so bad, even if I don't quite understand why it's necessary.

“Good morning, class,” I say, somewhat off-kilter. “Today we are going to be learning about the negative impacts of monocultures as it pertains to farming practices.”

Miles pipes up first. “Miss C., you keeping secrets from us?”

My brow furrows. “What do you mean, Miles?”

“You said you weren't dating. Who's the guy that kissed you when I walked in?”

And there it is. He sold the story to the tabloids.

“My roommate's brother,” I say, firmly believing it will help the situation.

It does not.

The gossip just got juicier, and the collective gasps can be heard from the international space station.

I manage to make it through first-period despite the

heightened interest in my non-existent love life, and by the end of the day, I've calmed down enough to think logically about the situation.

It would be one night out of ten glorious and adventurous days in Paris, France. I can pretend to date Sawyer for that.

As long as I don't kill him first.

FIVE

Sawyer

It took me two years to work my way up to sous chef at Catch 45, which is an impressive accomplishment considering I'm only twenty-four.

For the most part, I love my job. There are only a few things I hate.

The first thing I hate is that the head chef doesn't take suggestions when it comes to menu items.

The second thing I hate is that Georgia's school is on my way to work, and for some god-forsaken reason, I got it in my head that if I asked her in person, she would be more likely to say yes.

I wipe the back of my hand across my mouth before climbing into the driver's seat of my Jeep. I sit down and stare out into the high school parking lot, my hands firmly placed at ten and two.

All I'm thinking about is the way I *kissed* Georgia on

the cheek. I know she doesn't realize how much of a favor she's doing me—not yet, anyway. So, I guess I was trying to thank her, but I also knew something like that would infuriate her, too. Instead, she just stood there with her mouth hanging open like I had knelt down and asked her to marry me. She smelled like pears with a hint of peppermint.

I'm still staring out at the lot.

"What the fuck, Sawyer."

Great. I'm talking to myself. We are off to a fantastic start. I am now desperate and insane. What a combination.

I turn on the car and start navigating the shitshow that is the parking lot of Rosewood High School. When I finally make it onto the highway, I can't stop my mind from wandering.

Since asking Georgia to go with me to Paris, my mind has shown me all the different ways Anna could come back into my life.

I've pictured her showing up at the restaurant and barging into the kitchens. Fantasized about her driving all the way to my apartment to tell me she made a mistake. I even envisioned her stomping into the airport, short, shoulder-length brown hair wild as she demands I take her back.

God, I'm pathetic.

I try to shake off all thoughts of Anna, and when I get to the restaurant, my phone vibrates.

> **Emerson:** Mom's sick. I have class until eleven, but I'm going to pop over for lunch and help out. I'd tell you to bring food from the restaurant for dinner, but I'm not an asshole sister, so I'm going to ask nicely.

Emerson: Pretty, pretty please bring mom some food, loser.

Laughing at the text message, I type out a response of my own. If mom is sick, Dad will probably be lost when he gets home from work. I love my father, but the man's cooking skills consist of scrambled eggs and mac and cheese. Not that it's a problem, it just sucks to have only two options when you're sick. I'm sure mom will tire of the limited menu really quickly.

My mom loves to cook, and helping her in the kitchen was one of my favorite things growing up. Sandra Owens is the entire reason I decided to go to culinary school. I don't know if it started because I loved creating my own recipes or if I just loved cooking in general. Sometimes I think I fell in love with it all because it afforded me one-on-one time with my mom.

You know, being the oldest child and all that.

Me: Sure, Nemo. I'd be happy to, but it's going to cost you.

Emerson responds quickly, as she usually does when I use her childhood nickname. Well, I'm the only one that's ever really called her that.

Emerson: I literally hate you. What do you need?

When Emerson was nine, she broke her arm

climbing the tree in our front yard. When she got out of the hospital, she had a bright orange cast and one lame fin. Hence the nickname Nemo.

She pretends to hate it, but I distinctly remember the way she drew a striped design near her wrist that looked, oddly enough, like a clownfish. It could be a lot worse. I quickly type out my response, knowing I need to get back to the kitchen.

Me: I need Georgia's number.

Emerson sends me Georgia's contact information, including her school email and a fax number.

"A fax number?" I question aloud.

I'm surprised the contact didn't include explicit instructions on how to reach her via carrier pigeon.

I wince. Maybe that would have been better than showing up at her school the way I did.

Once Leo, the head chef, spots me, I push the question out of my mind and get to work. The restaurant isn't too busy on Mondays, but who am I kidding? Working in the restaurant industry is always busy. If I'm going to make it out in time to bring Mom some food, I'll need to bust my ass.

~

Consider my ass thoroughly busted. One of the line cooks was out, and I spent the entire night trying to fill in while Leo got on me about every last thing.

When I get out of my Jeep at my parents' house, my feet hurt, and I smell like fajitas.

I don't bother knocking because I texted Dad on the way over. He said Mom fell asleep on the couch nursing a box of tissues, but he must have said something about my plans to come over because when I turn into the living room, Mom is sitting up in the dim light of the television.

"Hey, ma." I kiss her temple, handing her the bag of food filled with a bowl of soup, a half-sandwich, and a side salad.

"No dessert?" she asks, and I can hear how congested she is.

I shrug, finding my way to my father's recliner and pulling the handle to stretch out and rest my tired feet.

"Beggars can't be choosers," I say with a wide smile. She laughs and starts setting things out on the coffee table.

"Emerson told me about Anna," she starts, and my stomach twists into a knot. I hadn't told my parents yet. Not that they liked Anna much. Don't get me wrong. My family will be kind to anyone I choose for myself, but I could tell after the first few months that something felt . . . off.

"Wow, for such a little person, Nemo sure has a big mouth." I rest my head on the back of the recliner and close my eyes. Maybe if she can't look at them, my mom won't realize how torn up I am over the Anna situation.

The breakup came out of nowhere.

"Are you okay, Sawyer? I know you liked that girl."

"Yeah, I'm fine, ma. No worries." *In fact, I have a fake girlfriend lined up anyway, and you'll love her. Actually, I'm pretty sure you already do.* I don't say that part out loud—mostly

44

because it sounds lame.

My mom loves Georgia, though.

I can't, for the life of me, figure out why that is.

"Where's Dad?" I ask, opening my eyes to see my mom hunched over the bowl of soup I brought.

"He went up to bed already. You know how it is around here. Getting sick is my only chance at a break. I have to milk it for all it's worth." A wide smile splits my mom's face, and I can see the wrinkles near her eyes and around her mouth. For fifty, my mom doesn't look too old, but I noticed some things changing over the past few years, and my heart clenches every time.

"I hate to be the worst son you've ever had, but I better get going home. It's already almost nine." I lower the footrest of the recliner and stand up, walking over to my mom to give her a hug.

"Oh, honey," she says. "You're the only son we have." She smiles then, looking up at me from the couch. "That makes you both the best son *and* the worst."

I huff a laugh before striding to the door. "Right." When my hand touches the knob at the front door, I turn back. "Night, ma. Let me know if you need anything."

She waves me off before telling me she loves me. I say it back because, well, you never know. When I was in high school, I didn't always say it, but after grandpa died, my dad got really finicky about everyone saying it back—always. By really finicky, I mean he turned into an actual monster and threatened your life if you forgot. Kind of counterproductive, but grief is funny sometimes.

When I get out to my jeep, I find my phone and pull

up Georgia's number. I'm not really sure what to say to her. I offered an explanation, but every time I think about what I'm having her do, it sounds ridiculous.

I haven't seen Warren in over a year, but he's been my best friend since the seventh grade. While we haven't kept in touch the way we should have, I know plenty about his soon-to-be wife, Sadie. I face-timed with Warren the night they got engaged. Sadie had the biggest smile and an even bigger rock.

I took one look at the ring and immediately knew I chose the wrong profession. Sous chef doesn't exactly allow you to purchase a ring the same price as a literal house.

I could see that she genuinely cares for Warren, though, and that's all that mattered to me.

I was, however, surprised to learn that Sadie's parents were paying for a small destination wedding in Paris. They completely funded our ten-day trip aside from food that isn't provided with the event or activities for those of us who are not in the bridal party. The wedding will be smaller, but I'd love to see the bill for something like that. I'm sure it would put my fifty-thousand-dollar salary to shame.

> **Me:** It's Sawyer. Thanks again for the feet pics, but unfortunately, I'd like a refund. When we talked first, you didn't mention the ghastly wart on your pinky toe.

Georgia texts back almost instantly. I haven't even finished laughing at my joke when the middle finger emoji pops up on my phone.

Georgia: Gross. I didn't know you had a foot fetish. What do you want?

I type out my response, delete it, and type it out again before I land on a final draft. Even then, I'm not sure it's a good enough explanation.

Me: I offered an explanation. Warren is an old friend of mine, but we don't talk the way we used to. I was just thinking, this is for his wedding, and it would make me a pretty shitty friend to show up with my relationship problems. It would be even shittier for me to show up sans girlfriend since they funded the trip. Wasting money and all that.

I watch the three bubbles appear. Disappear. Appear again.

I hate to admit it, but I'm anxious. If she doesn't agree to help me, I don't know what I'll do. I've waited this long to cancel, and if she doesn't come, Sadie's family will be out thousands of dollars.

Georgia: It's fine, Sawyer. I get it. Just keep your mouth to yourself. Especially with all the toes you're sucking to pad your fancy sous chef salary.

I can feel the press of her cheek against my mouth, and suddenly, her scent is in my nostrils. *Gross.* I wonder what she would say if she found out I make just about as much as she will as a teacher. I wouldn't want to admit that, though.

Me: I'm not sucking on anyone's toes. Though some PDA is to be expected. We have to be convincing.

The thought of holding Georgia Clark's hand makes me want to burn my own hand off. Cover it with gasoline and get rid of the entire limb.

It's going to happen, though. If we are going to convince Warren and Sadie of our relationship, we will have to, at the very least, be friendly with one another. My only saving grace is that Georgia will hate it. In that case, I can sacrifice a hand or two.

Georgia: If you wanted to hold my hand, Sawyer, maybe you shouldn't be such a grade-A ass wipe.

I stare at the text message, thinking back to a conversation from three weeks ago.

"I get that you're focused on your job, and that's fine, Sawyer. I'm even okay with the fact that you can occasionally be an asshole." Anna's voice is loud in my head. "I just don't think it's working anymore. This is the right thing."

I clear my throat, shifting uncomfortably as I turn the key and start my Jeep. Before I pull out of my parents' driveway, I send one more text to Georgia.

Me: I would rather jump into a pool of lemon juice with a thousand paper cuts all over my body, but a free trip to France is a free trip to France, so shut up and say thank you already.

SIX

Georgia

I'm going to kill him.

Shut up and say thank you already.

I can just hear Sawyer's deep condescending voice saying those words as if he's right next to me. My face feels hot. My chest feels like it's swelling with the force of all the anger inside of me.

I'm pretty sure I heard the same lemon juice and paper cut scenario thrown around during a first-grade game of *Would You Rather.*

And I would *rather* choke on a grape than engage in any sort of physical display of affection with Sawyer Owens. Especially after that stunt he pulled earlier today. I may have made it through Monday without any other classes mentioning what happened with Sawyer, but the high school rumor mill never quits turning. By tomorrow, I will be scrapping my lesson about sustainable farming and swapping it all for a new learning goal.

Students will understand that I, Georgia Clark, am not and will never be dating Sawyer Owens so that when given a five-paragraph essay assignment, they will be able to write a detailed explanation for why Sawyer is a complete and total dickface with one hundred percent accuracy based on a scoring rubric.

I chuckle to myself because my learning goal even has specific and measurable criteria. My professors would be so proud of me.

I find my way to the couch with my stack of papers and start grading while watching stand-up comedy on Netflix. The hope is that someone will tell enough jokes that I remember why I wanted this job to begin with.

That's a lie. I know exactly why I want this job. It's just not the paperwork.

When I was trying to choose a college major, I had tossed around a bunch of ideas relating to STEM, mostly because I felt like I was great at it. It was only after I fulfilled my volunteer hours with the elementary robotics club, I realized I might *actually* like teaching better than a job as a conservationist or something.

The funny thing is that most people assume teachers have favorite students, whether they like it or not. I have a funny view on that. Every student is my favorite at one time or another. It just depends on the day. It's also really hard to dislike a kid when you work so hard trying to get to know them.

Even my challenging students, the ones who don't really want to be there, eventually win me over.

Maybe I'm just easily swayed into liking people.

Not Sawyer, though.

If he were my student, I would lose my license after hosting a gladiator style competition in my classroom where I release different animals to eat him alive. The rest of the class would watch lions devour him—hopefully devouring the memory of that damn kiss, too.

I press my pen into the paper a little harder at the thought of the kiss. My cheek still stings from the touch. Not that Sawyer's lips weren't insanely soft, because they were. They were just equally disgusting. He probably gave me leprosy, the bubonic plague, at the very least, hives.

"You look distressed." Emerson walks into the living room with the bags of supplies she bought last Friday.

"I'm not," I lie. "What are you doing with all those craft supplies? You look like an Elementary Ed. Major."

Emerson laughs, tossing her hair over her shoulder. "It's supposed to be a fun challenge for one of my classes. Try to sell something using only the items you have lying around."

My brows furrow. "But you bought all of that this past weekend."

She smiles. "And people use Photoshop in marketing all the time. It's all a big lie. So, we didn't have pipe cleaners. I'm sure nobody will question it since I room with you."

I chuckle. "You do realize I'm becoming a high school teacher, right? We don't exactly use pipe-cleaners and macaroni noodles every day."

"Then you should really revamp your lesson plans, Georgia. You're going to bore your students."

I shake my head, returning to the stack of papers that

I swear has grown since I started.

I am dead inside.

Emerson works on her poster while I continue grading, and some new comedian cracks jokes in the background on the television.

Once I'm nearly done, and glitter and hot glue make up Emerson's new outfit my phone buzzes.

I reach for it, looking at the caller ID to see my mom's name flash on the screen.

"Hey, Mom!"

"Hey, sweetie!" In the background, our dog, Juniper, howls. My mom shushes her, and I hear water start to run. It's six-thirty there, and I'm sure she's just wrapping up dishes from dinner.

"Did you need something?" I ask, because Barb has gone silent—distracted by whatever tasks are in front of her.

"No, no. I was just calling to ask about your plans for spring break. You know, we're really going to miss you."

I think I hear tires skid outside. My stomach is in my throat as I try to piece together the easiest way to explain my situation to my mom. *Yeah, I scored a free trip to Paris with Emerson's brother. All I have to do is pretend to be his girlfriend, and I get free shit.*

What a freeloader.

It sounds even worse now. No matter how bad it sounds, I still need to tell my family where I'm going. If Sawyer actually kills me, I'd like them to know how it happened, or at the very least, where I was. Then they can launch a search for my body and give me a proper burial.

"Right," I drag out the word. "About that . . ."

Emerson's gone, off to the kitchen and making whatever midnight snack sounded best. She left her supplies on the floor. "So, I think I'm going to Paris."

It's silent.

I know exactly what my mother is thinking. I would think the same thing too.

With what money?

I can literally hear my bank account pleading with me, along with my bank, all of the bank tellers, the branch manager. Maybe even the corporate offices.

Good thing I'm not paying for the trip.

My parents are kind enough to help out here and there, but they don't really make much either, especially because they live in Portland and the cost of living is atrocious.

"I am very excited about this!" She's being genuine. "I just have some questions. Honey, how are you going to—"

"It's free," I interrupt. "Well, mostly. It's for a destination wedding. My flight and stay are covered, as is breakfast at the hotel. I just have to fund the rest of my meals and any activities."

"Oh, really!" I hear my mom adjust the phone. I can picture it clearly. Barbara Clark is standing at the kitchen sink with a damp towel over one shoulder, her apron on, and a phone stuck between her ear and the other shoulder. She always put her apron on to wash dishes because she couldn't help splashing water up on her shirt. My dad and I used to poke fun at her for it until one Christmas, Dad bought her an apron with sunflowers on it. She's used it ever since.

God, I really miss my family.

"Yeah, it's kind of a good deal. I think I can swing my other expenses, and I really need the break." A half smile tugs at my mouth. "I just wish it could be with you guys."

"Georgia, forget Portland! You're going to France. Oh my god, this is so exciting. I've always wanted to go to *Paris*. Who is getting married? College students don't have that kind of money."

I laugh because she's rambling now. "It's—" I don't have a good answer for this. I also don't see the point in lying to my mother about it—Sawyer plotting my death and all that. When they find my body, maybe they can cremate me instead. Scatter my ashes somewhere fun. "It's Sawyer's friend. You know Emerson's brother?"

"Oh." I can already hear her confusion, and honestly? *Same.*

Emerson walks in just in time to listen to my explanation. She folds her legs and sits on the floor with her elbows on her knees and her hands innocently placed under her chin. "Oh, I can't wait to hear this," she whispers.

I roll my eyes.

"Yeah, Sawyer had an extra ticket. I was going to be in the apartment alone for most of break, so *Emerson*," I emphasize my roommate's name, giving her a pointed look. "Decided it would be a mutually beneficial arrangement."

That sounds professional, doesn't it? No hint of anything. One other thing about Barbara Clark; she loves love, and her one and only daughter hasn't done a great job of providing any kind of romance to live vicariously through. I had a boyfriend in high school, and I dated a bit my freshman year. That's the extent of it, though.

When you're busy planning creative and innovative lessons to get high schoolers pumped about learning, you don't have time to date. Especially because high schoolers are generally not pumped about learning.

Like ever.

It's a very time-consuming challenge.

Couple that with the hours spent in class, the time I spend making worksheets to sell for some kind of income, and my senior project—

"Excuse me, sweetie." I already hear the question. "Sawyer Owens? Don't you hate him? Isn't he kind of an asshole?"

"Yes, yes, and yes," I say. "I know it sounds stupid, but it's a free trip to Paris."

"Are you sure it isn't—" She pauses. "Georgia, has something changed? Between you and Sawyer, I mean."

"No."

I gag. I actually gag and a little bit of vomit rises like the gates of hell stretched out before Sawyer when he reaches his untimely death—initiated by me, probably.

Emerson mouths *juicy* from her spot on the floor, and I've decided that she may be worse than a classroom of sixteen-year-olds. I point my finger into my mouth and pretend to continue gagging, just to emphasize my feelings about what my mother is suggesting.

"Like I said." I'm defending myself now. "Emerson suggested it. We will hardly see each other. I *do* have to pretend to be his date at the wedding, but aside from that, I get ten days to spend in Paris. It's a fair trade-off. I acted in that one play; I think I can do it."

"Georgia." My mom lets out a little laugh. "That play was a class requirement, and you feigned sick on the day of the performance."

Kind of rude for her to call me out so casually.

"Yeah, but that doesn't mean I was bad at acting. It'll be fine."

"Let me send you some money."

"Mom, no. No, Mom. That wasn't why I told you." I hate when my mother tries to send me money. My parents have good jobs, but they aren't loaded. Guilt sneaks its way into my chest like a tiny rodent curling up for the night.

"Gift-giving is my love language, so shut up." She adjusts the phone before I hear her yell, "Jason!" She's calling for my dad, and the guilt starts to fester. If she's asking Dad, then she's planning on sending more than fifty dollars.

"Mom, seriously. I can handle it. I just have to be careful about my budget."

I hear muffled voices in the background. At least they are calm. It still doesn't stop the entire situation from bothering me. College is expensive enough. I hate to ask more of people—more of my family.

"Dad says it's fine. We are going to send you six hundred."

"Six *hundred?*" I was not expecting that. "Mom, that's way too much."

"No, sweetie. It isn't. Dad got a bonus for his attendance at the warehouse. It's really nothing. We have it."

"Mom, seriously."

"Shut up, Georgia. I want you to have a good time."

"Mom." I fold into the couch, giving in because there's no way she's going to take no for an answer. I also don't want to be an ungrateful asshole, either. "Thank you."

There's a pause on the line before she starts talking again. "Um, Georgia?" Something in my mom's voice has me sitting up, my back straight. "Why did Sawyer agree to have you go again?"

"What do you mean? He had an extra ticket, and Emerson convinced him it would be a good idea. Why?"

"Georgia, you know you can ask for money if you need it. You don't need to be embarrassed."

My brow furrows, confusion weaving its web across my face. "You're already sending me money I don't need."

"*Feet pics?*"

Oh my god.

He's dead meat. He's deader than dead. Sawyer Owens will be thrown off the very peak of the L'Arc De Triomphe. It will be a long, long way down to the solid ground below. Maybe I'll find the guillotine and get all of us poor people to chant as we execute the wealthy—the wealthy being Sawyer, of course.

"That was a joke. I bought him a beer. He was paying me back."

"A fifteen-dollar beer?" She doesn't sound convinced.

Emerson looks like she's having the best day of her life. I can almost see tears in her eyes from the repressed laughter.

"It was a couple of beers," I lie, if only to get out of this conversation.

I'm not entirely sure why he sent me fifteen dollars, but I didn't bother finding out if it was a mistake. That was probably shady of me.

It was the very beginning of my freeloader lifestyle.

I wince, and my mom clears her throat. I wish the beige couch cushions would just swallow me whole.

"Right, a joke. Do people joke when they hate each other? Never mind." It's awkward now, and Emerson is practically rolling on the floor. "I sent over your money. Don't forget to call us from the Eiffel Tower! I want to feel like I'm there with you!"

"I'll be sure to call you every day. Love you, Mom." I'm glaring at Emerson, willing her to keep her laughter to herself if only for a few more moments. "And thanks."

"No problem, sweetie!"

As soon as the phone disconnects, Emerson erupts with laughter. Tears are streaming down her face, and she's clutching her side like she has the worst case of constipation the world has ever seen. "Your mom thinks Sawyer's taking you to France because you offered him pictures of your feet."

"She does not." I can't help it. Something about watching Emerson cackle like a hyena is pulling the laughter from me too. "I honestly think Sawyer looks worse when it comes to this. At least his joke is backfiring."

"You have to admit it was a good joke, Georgia. The only reason you hate it is because you hate him."

I laugh again. "Right. God, he's awful. Also, my feet are worth way more than fifteen dollars. How did you live with him all those years?"

"He's really not so bad. He likes to get under people's skin, but he's a good guy that cares."

I can hear the truth in her words, but I just can't seem to convince myself of whatever she's saying. For whatever reason, Sawyer decided I was the problem. Since the moment we met, he has insulted me at every possible turn.

I lean back against the couch, propping my feet up on top of the papers now stacked on the coffee table in front of me.

I release a sigh, holding my stomach because it's a little sore from laughing.

"I don't know how I'm going to make it through this trip."

"You're going to have fun," Emerson says as she picks up her hot glue gun and starts weeding through her craft supplies.

I should ask her if I can borrow it. Maybe I can hot glue Sawyer's mouth shut.

I offer her a half smile. "You're probably right."

SEVEN

Sawyer

I get off work earlier than usual since it's Friday, and I'm leaving for Paris tomorrow. I haven't texted Georgia, just confirming through Emerson that we are still on instead.

I'm actually starting to think this trip will be a good opportunity to get away for a while. I've been working my ass off since culinary school and have hardly slowed down to take a break. This will be my first real vacation in years.

When I get back to my apartment, I take time to water the snake plant I have near my sliding glass door. I'm surprised the thing is still alive. I hardly remember to take care of it.

Sitting on the couch and flipping the television on, I pull out my phone and find Georgia's name.

Me: Hey

I notice the bubble pop up almost immediately. She's probably freaking out about tomorrow. Emerson is a huge planner. She'd flip her shit if I waited this long to iron out details, and something about Georgia flipping her shit brings me immense joy.

Georgia: Still on for tomorrow. I'm taking an Uber.

I frown.

Okay, maybe she is unbothered. There's a small part of me that feels guilty having her take an Uber when I know how little money she's making. I'm not rich by any means, but I'm doing just fine.

Me: Save the money. I'll get you.

I expect her to turn down my offer immediately, but I figured I might as well try.

Georgia: Plotting my murder? Make sure you wear gloves. I'd hate for it to ruin your fancy career.

I roll my eyes, fighting the smile threatening to break through. *What is wrong with me?* I let her know that I'll pick her up around eleven-thirty since our flight leaves at one. We should get to Paris around ten in the morning their time, leaving us two hours before we can check into the hotel.

I drag myself off the couch, turning the television off before checking my bags one last time.

When I finally crawl into bed, I run through that last

scenario where Anna shows up at the airport to win me back. I even throw in a plot twist where she punches Georgia in the face, but it seems excessively mean, so I rewind the scenario and settle on a heated shove. It makes me feel like less of a douche.

~

"Could you pack a heavier bag?"

I'm hauling Georgia's monstrous-sized suitcase into the back of my Jeep while she stands there in her leggings, white sweatshirt, and jean jacket. Her curly hair is hanging around her shoulders, and she looks annoyed that I would insult her luggage choice.

Which is ridiculous since I'm the one putting it in the car for her.

"If I knew you would be the one piling it into your car, I would have made it heavier."

I turn around, looking down at her with a wide smile stretching across my face. "If you made it heavier, they wouldn't allow it on the plane. Then you could stay here."

"Are you uninviting me?" She raises a brow, lifting her travel mug of coffee and taking a drink. I watch her throat as she swallows, keeping the smile plastered to my face.

"I would never," I say, stomping around her to get in the car.

When Georgia gets into the passenger seat, she sets her cup of coffee in my cup holder and pulls the belt across her body.

I put my hand on the headrest and look back to pull out of the parking spot and make my way to the airport. She makes a show of throwing daggers at my arm stretched between us and tries to move away. I just smile.

Once we are on the road, I flick on the radio. It's still set to whatever gypsy jazz station I had playing earlier. It's what Leo plays in the restaurant's kitchen, and it kind of stuck.

I catch Georgia scowling from the passenger seat before she leans forward to turn the radio off. I scowl right back at her before turning my eyes to the road and flicking the station back on.

"Kind of rude when you have a guest in the car," she says, taking another drink of coffee.

"I'm trying to avoid talking to you right now," I say. It's mostly true. The reality is I don't even know what we would talk about. The scenario where Anna punches her in the face crosses my mind, and I huff a laugh.

"What's so funny?"

"Nothing." I look down at her mug and pull it from the cup holder to smell its contents.

"Hey!" she says, reaching for her cup.

"I'm just trying to figure out what's in this. Is there milk? You can't leave that shit in my car if there is." I put it back down in the cup holder and she folds her arms across her chest.

"I'll dump it or chug it before we get there. Don't worry." One corner of her mouth turns up, and I catch a glimpse of her hazel eyes flashing mischief. "Look how respectful I am of your car. I already make a great girlfriend."

I shift uncomfortably, gripping the steering wheel tighter. Warren texted me last night, and as it turns out, there are a few more events we will be required to attend besides just the wedding. I hope she doesn't hate me for springing all that on her now. I really need her to play nice.

"Speaking of," I start.

"Oh god, what?"

I chuckle at her dramatics. "Warren texted me last night. There's a dinner for all the guests that first night. We are going to have to go together." I smile at her, but she doesn't return it. "I hope you brought your acting skills."

"I thought it was just going to be the wedding?"

"There will be more than that, I assume. Not much, but it is a destination wedding. They didn't pay for our tickets and hotel without expectations of our presence."

Her nose wrinkles, and she slouches further into the seat of the car as I take the exit ramp. "Technically, they didn't pay for *me* at all."

There's silence, and Georgia's expression looks almost tight, like she's fighting off whatever emotion she's experiencing. Does she feel . . . *bad?* Is she even capable of that?

"Does someone feel guilty?" I finally ask as we pass the sign for the entrance to the airport.

"Maybe."

I raise my brows in surprise that she'd admit something like that to me. It almost makes her seem human. Almost. "Hey." I try to keep my tone gentle. I did picture my ex-girlfriend punching her in the face as part of a pre-sleep fantasy. I owe her a little kindness. "Don't worry about it.

The trip is going to be fun. I'm glad someone's coming with me."

"Of course you are." She leans her head back against the headrest, closing her eyes. "You get to watch me squirm while trying to figure out how to like you even a little for an entire dinner."

I can't help the smile pulling at my lips. There *is* some satisfaction in the thought of her acting like I'm not Satan incarnate, coming to earth and destroy her livelihood. For a second, I wonder what it would be like to have Georgia Clark treat me with kindness. I know she's capable since I see the way she treats my sister.

"There will also be a few hours before we can check into the hotel. I figure we can go see The Arch of Triumph. Then we can check-in, then attend dinner. After that, you're free of me."

She sighs, and her eyes are still closed when she talks. "The L'Arc de Triomphe   . You should at least try to say things correctly. Calling it The Arch of Triumph is disrespectful."

"So is saying *the* twice when you talk about it."

Her eyes crack open, narrowed into hazel slits. "You speak French?" she asks.

"No, you?"

"A little." Georgia shrugs. "Before I got crazy about science in high school, I took two years. If you need help finding the bathroom or ordering food, I can get us by."

"Impressive," I say, grabbing a ticket to park in the long-term parking lot before rolling up my window.

When I turn to look at her, she's staring at me with a

strange expression on her face. My brows furrow. It's strange to see Georgia do anything but scowl at me. She's been scowling since the horrid cookie incident on Thanksgiving.

"What?" I ask.

"Did you just compliment me?"

I grunt, turning toward the road as I drive away from the ticket dispensing machine. "Absolutely not."

"I think you did, Sawyer."

"I couldn't. You're horrible."

She laughs then, taking another drink of her coffee. "Keep that up, and your friend may actually think we are in love."

"Doubt it."

After we park and grab our bags out of the back, Georgia and I walk to security, where I hand her the plane ticket with her name on it. It was pretty easy to get it changed over after Emerson gave me all the information to do it.

We make it through the long security line seamlessly and then kill a few hours playing on our phones by our gate.

When we board the plane, I can feel the nerves setting in. Maybe Georgia had the right mind to be guilty about coming on this trip. I'm lying to one of my best friends. A week ago, it seemed like a good idea, but now it seems almost as shitty as wasting a couple thousand dollars.

It doesn't matter though. When I help Georgia put her carry-on in the overhead storage bin, she says thank you and finds her spot by the window. I check my ticket again, noting that she actually has the aisle seat on this flight. We have a layover in New York where we will board an even larger plane, and I'm fairly sure we are both in a center section for that ride.

"That's not your seat," I say.

"You're really going to deny your girlfriend the window seat?" There is no mercy on Georgia's face. Not a single ounce of it. There is, however, the slightest lift to the corner of her full mouth, making her look amused.

I cock an eyebrow at her in challenge. "Don't test me."

Georgia just laughs and settles in as I find my spot near the aisle.

At least I'll be closer to the restroom. I suppose it's not all bad. I do wish I had the better view out the window.

When the plane takes off, I rest my head on the back of the seat, settling into the comfortable silence that will be the next thirteen hours.

EIGHT

Georgia

If Sawyer Owens is good at anything, anything at all, it's sleeping on airplanes.

In fact, Sawyer Owens slept almost the entire thirteen hours. I'm not sure he was even awake for our layover, and something about it irritates me because I was up the entire time.

I think I watched every movie available on the flight and still had time to listen to *Taylor Swift's* entire discography. So, by the time we land at the *Charles de Gaulle* airport, my eyes feel like an actual desert.

During a drought.

On a very windy day.

As wildfires take over the landscape.

"I think I need eyedrops," I say as Sawyer focuses on following the signs to baggage claim. I'm certain he hears me, but he doesn't respond. The man just power walks like he is trying to run away from me. I'm taking at least five steps to his one and pulling my carry-on behind me.

"Sawyer!" I am dreading the moment I have to peel my contact lenses out of my eyes. I'm so tired that they're probably all sticky and fused to my cornea. I really should have worn my glasses on the plane.

"What?" Sawyer stops and turns around. He seems irritated, though I can't imagine why. He should feel reborn after the rest he got.

"I need to buy some eyedrops or stop and put on my glasses before we leave."

"Glasses?" he questions.

I grunt, folding my arms across my chest. "Do you think there's a place to stop?"

"Probably."

He's just standing there staring at me—unhelpful.

I hope both sides of his pillow are warm tonight—scorching, even.

"Okay, well. Can we stop somewhere?"

"Sure." He turns around, rushing to the baggage claim again as I struggle to keep up. All I hear are the wheels of my carry-on sliding across the tile floor of the airport and the shuffling sound my backpack makes every time I take a step.

Sawyer manhandles our bags as he pulls them off the conveyor belt. Without a word, he's charging for the exit. I don't know what has gotten into him, but I can't imagine it's much. Maybe he had a bad dream where he finally realized all of his terrible qualities and grappled with feelings self-loathing.

I grab his arm, forcing him to stop and look at me. I'm pretty sure most of the cells in my hand died at the connection, and I quickly let go once I have his attention.

"What has gotten into you?" I ask. "You slept nearly the entire way here. I'm exhausted. Why are you acting so—" I don't have a word, so I just gesture to all of him and hope he gathers my meaning. By the way his brows crease together, I'm certain he's clueless.

Figures.

"What do you mean?"

"What do you mean, what do I mean? You're plowing through the entire airport like a bulldozer. What has you so worked up?" My face scrunches up in disgust thinking about all the *what-ifs*. Like, what if this is Sawyer's natural personality coming out to shine?

"I was just thinking."

"A first." I toss the barb out with little consideration, and Sawyer runs a hand down his face, already fed up with me.

We are off to a great start.

"I don't want you posting about the trip on social media."

"What the *hell?*" I am pretty sure I almost shriek in frustration—like a cat. "You can't tell me I can't post photos of *my* trip to Paris. I'm also not sure why you'd even care or why this would be an issue, to begin with."

"Don't be such an ass." The insult takes me aback for a second. "I'm not trying to boss you around. Just don't post any photos with *me* in them."

"Isn't that a little suspicious?" I ask. "Our social

media accounts are already completely void of one another. Do you think Warren will check them?"

"Don't you think Anna will check them?"

"Oh." *Oh.* So, that's what this is about. He doesn't want his ex-girlfriend seeing him bring another girl along on *their* trip. If only she knew our actual feelings for one another.

"Oh," he says by way of explanation, and then he's back to stomping his way through Paris. What a fantastic and respectful arrival. I'm sure the entire country is happy to have him.

We find a small store in the airport that sells rewetting drops for my contact lenses, and I find myself praying to the CEO of whatever company sells them because my eyes have never been more thankful.

Sawyer secures a taxi for us and helps load up my bags without a word. I can tell he's still in a mood—lost in his own thoughts, I suppose.

We get into the taxi and Sawyer asks the driver to take us to the L'Arc de Triomphe. I can't say I'm pleased to walk around the monument with all my bags, but since the hotel isn't ready for us, I don't really have a choice.

It's silent in the cab, and Sawyer has his head resting on the headrest in the backseat. I sincerely hope he's not about to fall asleep again. Speaking of which, I am still exhausted. I can feel myself drifting as the taxi moves through traffic. There will be time to take in the scenes later, so I let myself close my eyes.

At least I hope there will be time.

As long as it isn't all spent attending wedding activities.

Speaking of which—

"What about the photos?" My eyes snap open.

"Huh?" Sawyer turns his head to look at me without lifting it. His eyes are dead, just like his soul.

"The wedding photos. What happens when they post wedding photos, and we are in them together?"

He sighs. "I hadn't thought that far."

"Of course you didn't. If you were so worried about Anna finding out you brought another girl, you really should have thought about that before you asked me to—"

"God! Would you *shut up*, Georgia?"

I'm staring at him and blinking. Something about the way he said it, the way it came out all loud and annoyed. It shouldn't bother me, but it does. I fight off whatever thing is twisting in my chest and making it feel sore. I think my lack of sleep is making me sensitive. Without another word, I turn and face forward until the taxi drops us off.

I rush to the back to grab my own bags without Sawyer's help, and before he can say anything, I'm walking faster than he did at the airport, hightailing it to the beautiful arch ahead of me. It's hard to see though because I'm blinking back tears.

I'm not usually overly emotional, but I can't help thinking this was a bad idea. We just landed, and already Sawyer is yelling. I don't have the money to purchase a ticket home. The entire ground looks like it's tilting because I'm so tired. I just need to get away from him.

"Georgia, wait."

I don't stop. If I'm going to be stuck here, I might as well enjoy my time. I rush to get closer to the arch. I won't be able to go inside, though. For one, I still have my bags. For two, it costs money. I'm not willing to blow through my spending money just because Sawyer is a rude and selfish dickwad.

"Georgia."

He catches up to me, and before I know it, he's blocking my path, his body stationed right in front of the magnificent carvings decorating Napoleon Bonaparte's attempt at compensating for his height.

Sawyer is not like Napoleon. At least I'm not crying. My eyes got a little salty, but not a single tear fell. I hope I just look pissed. "You're blocking my view, dickhead."

He doesn't move. Sawyer just stares at me with his bags and his stupid gray joggers, and his stupid black sweatshirt, with his stupid, *stupid* face.

"I'm sorry."

"Not good enough." I stick my chin out, hoping he can feel how much I hate him. I hope my hate for him is so thick, so palpable, that he chokes on it and falls dead on his first day in Paris.

"You're being a baby."

"Wow," I scoff, folding my arms across my chest. "A real charmer, this one. You know, the baby insult really kind of negates the entire apology you were going for just a moment ago."

"Look, Georgia. I am sorry. It hasn't been long since Anna—"

I hold up a hand to stop him. "It's fine. I don't want to hear about your sad boy relationship problems." Even though I've used the rewetting drops, and even though I'm no longer fighting off tears, the whole world seems just a little too blurry. I can feel exhaustion hit me like one of the airplanes we rode on, and I sway on my feet a little, putting my hand on my suitcase to catch myself.

"Hey." Sawyer reaches out, putting a hand on my shoulder before snatching it back as if he thought better of it. "Are you okay?"

"Yeah, I'm fine. I just think I need to sit down." I don't wait to find a spot and sit myself right on top of my suitcase. The thought hits me that we are just below the L'Arc de Triomphe in Paris, France. The entire thing kind of makes me dizzy.

"Are you sure you're fine?"

"I think I'm just tired," I say, because it's the truth, though I don't forget to remind myself of how needy I'm sounding. *Get me eye drops! I'm so tired, I think I may pass out!* "I didn't really sleep on the plane, and I didn't eat much either."

Sawyer's brows pull together. "Do you want to go get some food? We have a few hours before check-in, but I'm sure there's something close by."

I want to tell him no. I want to tell him no, stand up and walk away like the big girl I am, but I don't. Instead, I turn my head away from him and mutter, "sure."

Before I know it, we are walking again, and I'm fighting to keep my head on straight. I really should have slept on the plane. I've been up for twenty hours already.

I sit outside of a small sandwich shop, and Sawyer grabs me something to eat. I think he's trying to make up for the way he yelled at me. The way the words stung has me even more confused. He was only telling me to shut up.

I don't think too hard on it before he walks out with two of the biggest, fanciest sandwiches I've ever seen.

"Here," he hands me one and sits in the chair across from me, taking a bite.

"I'm sure you're thinking of all the ways you could make a better sandwich than this." I shove the sandwich in my mouth, and somehow, I highly doubt he could make anything half as good. That may just be the starvation talking.

"You know," he starts. "You really are already making this a drag."

"Thanks," I say around a mouthful of food.

Sawyer's expression changes and becomes more serious. "Look," he starts. "I really am sorry."

I nod once, refusing to talk about it at all. I think maybe the jet lag is getting to me.

"You really didn't sleep?" he asks.

"No," I say. "You did, though. At one point, I had to shove you off of me. Kind of gross."

He laughs and grabs a napkin from the table. I didn't even see him bring those over with the food. "Sure," he supplies.

"You were! Didn't you wonder why you woke up with that shiner under your eye?"

"Ha, ha. Very funny." He offers me a clean napkin, and I take it from him, wiping my mouth before I continue to scarf down whatever masterpiece he found me.

"We can probably head to the hotel soon. We should have a cab waiting. You'll definitely want to sleep before dinner tonight."

I sigh. "My sleep is going to be so messed up."

Sawyer is licking his lips and rolling up the paper from his sandwich. My eyes track the movement, noticing how soft his mouth looks.

"Think of it this way," he begins. "If you sleep during the day, then you won't have to use the pull-out. We can just share the bed."

My eyes flick to his, and I can feel my face getting warm.

What the fuck?

"You know," he barrels on, catching his mistake. "We can take shifts. I'll just have the cleaning staff burn the old sheets after you sleep on them."

I shake off whatever weird haze I was in and put a small smile on my face. "Burn the *mattress*."

Sawyer offers me a wide smile before saying, "Exactly."

I finish my sandwich and watch people walking down the street. I think maybe my mind got a little muddied by his kindness.

When I finish my food, we set off to find our cab, and I notice I feel better. I cannot, however, wait to enter a coma when we get back to the hotel.

NINE

Sawyer

Georgia fell asleep so fast that I'm disappointed I didn't document it. I'm certain she would have broken a record, and I could be making millions by now. Which would be helpful, considering I already paid for her cab and sandwich. Which she didn't even bother to thank me for.

I exit our room and find my way to the elevators. The tiled floors give the hotel a more expensive appearance—all sleek lines and modern black and white design. Georgia is probably having the time of her life—practically a homeless woman I adopted and decided to take to France.

I don't really have a plan for how to spend the day, but I noticed a café close by where I could get coffee and something to eat.

Pressing the button, I wait for the elevator, my mind tracing over everything that hit me as we landed.

This was a stupid decision.

I can still see Anna's face when she ended things, the way her blue eyes held no emotion—held an emptiness. The image played over and over in my mind on the plane ride, and for the first time in a month, I started to touch on the wound she left.

I couldn't help trying to piece together everything I might have done wrong. It's not like I don't know that I can be an asshole. Emerson makes sure I don't forget it, but there's never any heat behind her words. Anna said it before she left, but having Georgia throw it in my face every chance she gets really puts the spotlight on my deficiencies.

I started thinking through ways I could fix myself— our relationship—pondering how I could win her back. That doesn't make sense, to begin with, because it's been four weeks, and I haven't heard from her. Still, I couldn't stop over-analyzing this trip and wondering what would happen if she saw me bringing another girl along. If she got the wrong idea.

Then there's the incessant reminder that I should probably feel worse than I do. Sorrow should be my favorite adjective, but it just . . . isn't.

I run my hand down my face as the elevator opens to the large lobby of our hotel. We are so close to the Eiffel Tower; I can't imagine how much Sadie's family spent on this place. Every inch of the lobby displays clean lines and white tile. There are purple accents that match the one wall in our room upstairs.

"Sawyer?"

I turn around at the familiar voice—one I haven't heard in a long time. "Hey man, how are you?" I say, drawing

Warren in for a quick hug. He's filled out considerably, all muscle and wide smiles. It doesn't take long for me to see the happiness radiating off him, and I try my best to shove all my problems aside. I'm not about to ruin his wedding.

"Good, good. Where's your girl?" he asks, dark eyes lighted in anticipation.

"Oh." I clear my throat, reminding myself that my girlfriend is Georgia, and Georgia is my girlfriend. "She's upstairs sleeping. I guess the flight was a bit rough."

"Oh really? That's a shame. I was really hoping to meet her." Warren shoves his hands in his pockets, looking around the lobby. "Sadie should be down soon. By soon, that could mean the next five minutes or the next thirty."

I laugh, thankful the conversation has strayed from my fake girlfriend. I haven't talked to Georgia about it, but I'm going to need to make sure she knows a little something about me. Especially for tonight.

"Hey, well, I don't mean to keep you waiting. We will see you at dinner anyway." Warren runs a dark hand over his cropped hair and offers me a wide smile. "I seriously can't wait to meet her."

"Yeah, of course." My smile is half-assed, and I know it. My heart is racing, and I'm hoping Warren isn't suspicious. I'm going to need to work on my acting skills. "I'm going to go grab her some coffee for when she wakes up," I add, hoping to play up the doting boyfriend role.

"She already has you wrapped around her finger then." Warren lets out a casual laugh. "The café close to the hotel does some pretty cool latte art. You should get her something from there. I'm sure they have whatever she drinks."

Who knows? I think. *It's not like I've gotten her coffee before.*
"I'll have to check it out."

"This is going to be super rude," Warren starts, "but what is her name again? We haven't talked in a while. I want to say it starts with an A?"

The color drains from my face. I'm sure of it. "Georgia," I choke out. "Her name's Georgia."

"Wow, I'm such an ass. You're going to have to tell me about her before dinner. I don't want it to look like I haven't paid attention."

I fight through all the things that I could say about her, trying to land on the ones that are true. If I stick to the truth, it'll make everything else run more smoothly. Once we have to start keeping track of lies, it'll complicate things, and the idea of that sends guilt running through me. I don't want to lie to Warren any more than necessary.

God, this was a terrible idea.

"Georgia's student teaching at a high school. Environmental Science," I provide. "I think you'll like her." That part isn't a lie. Georgia can be kind when she wants to be, and funny. She really *is* funny. I'm sure Warren will appreciate her sense of humor.

Warren pats me on the back. "Great, man. Well, we are really glad you could be here. Since the wedding is in six days, we will have to hang out beforehand. Maybe it'll help with the stress Sadie's feeling. Her mom likes to plan. Not in a helpful way, though. Rachel is more like a bulldozer when it comes to what she wants for the wedding."

"Yeah, we'd love to hang out." I hate myself for

saying it. I already hate myself. I've just committed more of my time to pretending. Georgia is going to kick me in the balls. Maybe I should find a place that sells protection for my genitals. Knowing Georgia, she wouldn't stop at one kick. She'd probably keep going until I couldn't have kids. I wince just thinking about it.

When Warren walks away, I'm left to ponder the damage I may have done. We didn't commit to anything. All I said is that we would love to hang out before the wedding. Which we *will* do—at dinner tonight.

I walk my way over to the café and struggle to order. At the sandwich place, the employee spoke some English, and I could get by with pointing and smiling. Here, there's no coffee to point to.

I spend some time sitting by the window and watching people walk past, surprised to see the city filled with way more tourists than I expected.

Before I leave, I go back up to order something for Georgia. It's way harder than I thought—especially because I don't know what the fuck she actually drinks.

My mind goes back to when I stopped by Rosewood High School. She smelled like pears and peppermint.

I settle on a latte with some peppermint flavoring and walk my way back to the hotel.

TEN

Georgia

I'm blinking up at the ceiling, feeling much better when I hear the door creak open.

Sawyer walks in, and I feel my cheeks flush. I can't say that I'm not embarrassed about earlier. In fact, I am incredibly embarrassed.

I sit up and reach over to pull on my glasses. My hair is piled on top of my head, and I'm positive I have lines across my face from how hard I was sleeping. I was dead to the world—one millimeter away from identifying as a ghost.

When he gets further into the hotel room, I notice Sawyer is carrying a coffee cup in one hand. He looks more relaxed, and I hope he did something to get rid of his bad attitude. It would be completely unfair if I were the only one working toward bettering myself on this trip. Granted, all I did was take a nap.

"I thought you might want some coffee before

dinner." Sawyer hands me the cup, and it's still hot.

"That was—" I blink once—twice. "Nice. Thank you." I clear my throat. If we are going to make it through a meal with his friends, I should probably start treating him like a human being instead of the steaming pile of dog shit he actually is. "And thank you for the cab ride, the sandwich, and for not judging me."

He grunts, turning around to pull off his sweatshirt. I catch a flash of skin above the waistband of his joggers. My eyes flick away briefly.

"Don't worry, I was definitely judging you." He straightens his t-shirt and looks at me with a smile splitting his face. "Between the peanut butter and jelly sandwiches, and how emotional and needy you get when you're tired, I'm starting to question if you may actually be a toddler."

"And just like that, your kindness is eclipsed by your absolute douchery."

"That's not a word."

"Maybe." I grin up at him. "Maybe it's just French, and since you don't speak the language, you will never know."

He huffs a laugh, throwing the sweatshirt over the desk chair in our hotel room.

When we got here, I didn't have time to look around. It's a fancy hotel, but there isn't a couch in our room. There's a desk next to the dresser and a few uncomfortable-looking chairs by the balcony overlooking the city. I wonder if we could order a cot.

I pull off the lid of my latte to test how hot it's going to be. When the lid comes off, I notice an expertly done heart crafted in foam and espresso. "Uh, Sawyer. Why is there a heart in my latte?"

He's digging around his suitcase and pulling out clothes and toiletry items. "Because this place is fancy. What do you mean?" He seems a little irritated, and I can't express how much satisfaction it brings me.

"Sawyer," I say. "This is really sweet, but I think you're taking the fake girlfriend thing too seriously." I smell the subtle scent of peppermint permeating above the drink and fight off a groan of happiness. At least he got my coffee order right.

"Fine," he says, prowling over to the bed. Sawyer places his fists on the mattress and leans in so we are at eye level. I hold the coffee between us as a form of protection, blowing over the top to cool it down. "Next time," he continues, "I'll have them make a picture of a giant dick."

He smirks as if he made the best joke of the century and walks over to get whatever he pulled out of his suitcase. I have to admit it was pretty good, but I can probably top it.

"Cool," I respond. "You can snap a picture of the latte art for your *Pinterest* board." I raise an eyebrow. "You know, the one titled *Big Dick Goals and Inspiration.*"

To my surprise, he laughs. Sawyer Owens actually laughs, and not the condescending irritated laugh he typically offers me. This laugh sounds like he really finds me funny.

"Did you just laugh at me?" I ask, fighting a smile. I don't want to appear too happy about it. He needs to know I still hate him.

"It was kind of funny," he supplies.

Something about him calling me funny has my

stomach doing a weird flip. I don't like it. "No, it wasn't." I furrow my brows, setting my coffee down on the nightstand. "You're gross."

"And you're right," he says. "I'm going to take a shower before dinner." He walks over to the door of the bathroom and looks back at me. His brown eyes are lit with amusement, and I know he's about to say something he's *really* proud of. He'll probably tell me my eyes look like soggy seaweed. "Don't think too hard about my dick."

"Oh my god, ew!" I grab a pillow, tossing it toward him, but he deflects it easily. "That's disgusting!"

He's laughing when he disappears into the bathroom, and I'm left alone to sit with my thoughts.

After a moment, I take another sip of my latte as a warm feeling washes over me. I'd like to say it's the drink, but I'm definitely picturing that small sliver of skin Sawyer flashed when he took off his sweatshirt.

"Ew, weird," I whisper to myself before turning my thoughts to literally anything else.

I settle on the safest thought I can think of:

The latte is pretty good.

ELEVEN

Sawyer

I'm sitting on the end of the bed in the hotel room, and I cannot sit still.

The only thing worse than showing up and ruining your friend's wedding with relationship drama is having your friend find out you lied about a relationship to offer your sister's best friend a free trip to France.

I could possibly be a trash human being. I am most likely trash.

Georgia comes out of the bathroom with her hair damp and legs out. Her black dress is shorter than I anticipated. It wouldn't be offensive for dinner. It's actually perfect. I just didn't expect it to look like this.

My thoughts scramble.

Good. It looks good.

I swallow and drag my eyes away from her as she uses a towel to scrunch up her hair.

"Should we call down and order a cot or something?"

"What?" I say, turning back to her. The dress has sheer sleeves with some kind of design and a deep v-neckline. I don't think I could strain any harder to keep myself looking at her face.

This is Georgia, here. I'm trying to remind myself of all the ways she literally sucks.

Not a great word choice.

Oh god.

Georgia deadpans, and the annoyed look on her face saves me from my misery.

"I don't know if you noticed," she starts, "but there's no pull-out couch in this hotel room. I'm not about to sleep on one of those rock-hard chairs in the corner by the balcony."

"Oh," I say, fighting the urge to smile. "That's not a problem. You can just sleep on the floor."

The floor is definitely a good choice. Maybe she can put her farmer overalls back on.

She scoffs. "Such a gentleman."

"Hey, I brought you coffee." I'm pointing at her, my brows raised. I lower my hand but try to emphasize my point. "That was pretty nice."

"You did," she admits. "It even had the heart on it. You're really trying at this whole boyfriend thing."

The nerves start going again, and I can't stop my legs from bouncing. "Speaking of which, I think we need to talk about some things before dinner."

Georgia is digging around in her bag, and I'm forced

to look up at the ceiling. She's bending over. Is her dress even long enough for that? Maybe she should put on some slacks and a white button-down like me.

Sawyer, you're being an idiot.

"What is there to talk about? I'll just hold your hand and look at you like I want to jump your bones. Easy."

What the actual fuck?

I try not to choke on my saliva. If we are going to be convincing, she has to get to know me. At least a little.

"I think you should probably know some basics since they'll ask questions." I don't stop to wait for a response and just plow forward, rattling off facts about myself she may need to know. "I went to culinary school for four years, worked my way up to sous chef at Catch 45. My favorite color is blue."

"Classic," she interrupts.

I roll my eyes, trying to think of something to throw her off. "I enjoy knitting."

"What?" She stopped applying whatever makeup she was using to look at me.

"I'm joking." One corner of my mouth quirks up before she turns back to the mirror above the desk. "I was just making sure you're paying attention. I like hiking and kayaking."

"Outdoorsy," she says while getting something else out of her makeup bag.

I chuckle, leaning back on my hands while I wait for her to finish up. The dinner is supposed to be in the hotel. I guess they have a private room with multiple tables. Warren texted me to let me know we would be sitting with them.

Apparently, Sadie's mom is driving her crazy, and they need a change. Plus, he wanted to catch up. It's been too long.

Georgia turns to me again, squaring her stance. "Aren't you going to ask anything about me?"

I look her up and down, fighting the urge to actually take in what I'm seeing. I hope she thinks I'm judging her.

"What is there to know?" I supply. "You're becoming an environmental science teacher. You have curly hair. Your favorite color is probably green, and you buy shitty cookies from the store, even though the recipe for sugar cookies is painfully simple."

"Wow." She's annoyed. I can feel it. "You don't even know my parents' names or *my* hobbies."

She has a point. "Okay, what are they?"

"Barbara and Jason. They're still married. And I, too, enjoy hiking and kayaking. I grew up in Portland. The Pacific Northwest has great trails."

I nod. It would be pretty cool to check out the trails on that side of the country. I've never been.

"Great," I say, standing up from my spot on the bed. "I think we can just wing the rest."

I'm pushing toward the door when she pulls something else out of her bag and starts tracing a line around her eyes.

"How long is that going to take?"

"Five minutes," she says. Putting the liner away.

"You look fine." I'm itching to get out of this hotel room. The nerves are too much to handle, and I'm tired of looking at Georgia in her damn dress. "Let's just go."

She puts some kind of Chapstick on her lips and

turns to look at me. She's dead serious. "Don't you want your girlfriend to look better than *fine*? They have to believe you're actually attracted to me."

She zips up her makeup bag and takes a step toward the door. I grab her arm gently to usher her forward, leaning down to get closer to her ear. "Trust me," I say. "They won't question it."

Georgia looks stunned as I yank the door open, release her arm, and we head out into the hallway. She's a few steps behind me but quickly catching up.

"Right," she says, and I can see the confusion on her face. I can't help but smirk. "I hope this isn't too fancy."

I shrug. "How should I know?"

~

Dinner is fancier than I expected, but not uncomfortably so. I don't feel underdressed, and Georgia picked the right outfit for the occasion, but should still have worn literally anything else. A respectable parka would have done the job nicely.

We meet Warren at the entrance, and he takes us back to a nice room with round tables scattered about. The white tablecloths and centerpieces make me wonder exactly what Sadie's parents do.

Warren was in school to become a civil engineer, so I know he makes enough. I kind of hated that he moved all the way to Nevada for his job after college. It would have been nice to have him around. Though few people stayed in Michigan after school. I just wanted to be close to my family.

Before we sit down, Warren's fiancé, Sadie, gets up to greet us. She pulls Georgia into a tight hug, and I'm thankful that my fake girlfriend doesn't seem repulsed by the physical touch. She's a natural.

"It's so nice to meet you," Sadie says, her warm brown skin glowing in the dim lights of the restaurant. "Warren has told me so much about you, Sawyer." She's looking at me now. "I think he misses being close by."

I chuckle as she draws me in for a hug, too. Georgia plasters a smile on her face, and I am almost convinced that she *wants* to be here.

"It would be nice to have him around again," I say.

Sadie steps away. "Oh, you two should definitely visit Nevada sometime." Georgia is giving me a wide-eyed look, one laced with the tension of: *Absolutely not. No way. Not happening.*

We all take our seats before Sadie continues talking. "We are really glad to have you here. Seriously. I can't wait to spend some time with you both before the wedding. Georgia, Warren was just telling me about you."

For a moment, my heart picks up in my chest. I have no idea what she's going to say.

"He says you're studying to become a teacher?" Sadie is looking right at Georgia as Warren rests a hand on her chair. They look comfortable—natural. Georgia and I are sitting miles apart. I scoot my chair closer. If she notices, she doesn't say anything.

"Yeah, I'm student teaching now. It's Environmental Science. I really enjoy it, but there's a lot of work involved outside of the classroom. I'm thankful to be here for your wedding." She's still smiling, and I'm wondering if maybe our faces will hurt by the end of this. At least she doesn't have to lie about her job or anything. "I did have to bring papers to grade while I'm here."

"Oh, well, I'm sure Sawyer will help you with that. He's a pretty generous guy, from what I've heard."

Georgia's hazel eyes flick to me, and I can see all the layers behind her gaze. I'm hopeful Sadie and Warren don't see it, too. "Yeah," she says. "He is."

Something softens in her face, and I almost believe she means it.

Put this woman on Broadway.

"So, what is it you do for work, Warren?" Georgia asks.

Warren laughs as the waitress comes around and takes our drink order. There are multiple servers, and I can see Warren's parents sitting on the other side of the room, with whom I assume to be Sadie's parents as well.

When the waitress leaves, Warren continues. "I'm a civil engineer. I'm surprised Sawyer hasn't talked about me at all. It's a little offensive." There's nothing off in his tone, just casual conversation with a hint of sarcasm.

Internally, though, I'm cursing myself for not thinking about telling Georgia about Warren. I'm on the edge of my seat, waiting for her response.

"Oh, you know how it is," she starts. "He's told me loads." I pull the glass of water to my lips, taking a drink. "I'm just too distracted by his body to listen to a word that comes out of his mouth."

I choke on my drink, quickly grabbing a napkin while

coughing. Warren and Sadie laugh like Georgia didn't just spew the most ridiculous lie all over the fancy table.

When our waitress gets to us, I notice the French accent, and I'm thankful that the staff speaks English. Georgia might be right about the language making things more difficult. It was damn hard to order her that ridiculous coffee.

I go with whatever pasta they had on the menu, unable to read most of it. It's somewhat frustrating because I could stand to take notes on the cuisine here.

When our food comes, our table becomes quieter, and I note the way Warren is holding Sadie's hand beneath the table. Maybe we aren't convincing enough.

I lean over to whisper to Georgia. "I think maybe you're laying it on too thick. You don't need to lie about my body."

She swallows, keeping her eyes on her food while she twirls her fork. "Lying?" she says. "You look just fine, Sawyer. It's not exactly unbelievable that I'd find you attractive."

That stuns me.

I sit up, straightening in my chair and letting the words marinate. It's as close to a compliment as she's ever given me.

I'm still watching the way Warren and Sadie are touching. She has her hand on his leg while they eat and talk to one another. You can tell they are clearly in love.

I lean over again. "I'm going to hold your hand now."

Georgia laughs quietly. "Honestly, Sawyer, I don't

think you're laying it on thick *enough*."

I scoot closer. "Fine," I say, wrapping my arm around the back of her chair and resting my hand on her shoulder. Her back is stiff, and I can tell she wasn't expecting that kind of contact.

I lean in, just to make it more convincing. My mind is circling back to her compliment, remembering the way I couldn't stop looking at her dress when she walked out of the bathroom. There's no denying Georgia is beautiful. Even if her personality swoops in to ruin it.

She's not so bad. She's handling herself well at this dinner and making things easy on you.

I try to kick the thought out of my head as my lips come close to her ear. I can feel her hair tickling my cheek as I speak. "Is this thick enough?" I ask, lowering my voice. I can feel the way she shivers, and it sends something warm shooting down my spine. "Shall I tell you all about my hot body while we sit here? Make you squirm a little."

I lean away and note the way her hazel eyes are blazing, looking almost green in the light.

Georgia shifts in her chair, pulling the skirt of her dress lower on her thighs. This time, I let myself track the movement.

"Ease up, would you?" she practically hisses, but I can tell she wasn't completely immune. I keep my face close.

"Whatever you say, Princess."

When I sit back up, I keep my arm draped casually around the back of her chair. I can tell she feels off balance, and I have to admit I do, too.

Something about the dress, and the way Warren is

smiling at us, makes me think we were a little too convincing. I could almost imagine myself being attracted to Medusa herself.

You are attracted to her.

I wince, taking a bite of the pasta and hoping that we can make it through dinner without alerting our company that the entire thing is a sham.

When I shift in my chair, trying to hide that I liked our conversation more than I let on, I stop worrying so much.

Pretending may be easier than I thought.

TWELVE

Georgia

I hate myself.

I could not hate myself more. Especially as we walk back to our room, and I can't get the memory of Sawyer's hot breath ghosting over my neck out of my head. I can't stop replaying his words over and over. My body is too hot and confused. He's an asshole, and I hate him.

But I also hate myself.

I loved Sadie and Warren, though. After my weird conversation with Sawyer, we talked about all the activities there are to do around the city. Apparently, Versailles is only an hour away, and I desperately want to go and tour the palace and the gardens. I'm thinking about finding a time to get a car and go.

The only downside to the kindness of Sawyer's friends is that I accidentally agreed to a cooking class with them.

Tomorrow.

And with Sawyer.

Did I mention I hate myself?

"That went well." Sawyer is walking next to me, and I forgot how much taller he is. I'm carrying my heels in my hand, making my way to our room.

The rest of the dinner was simple enough, but I was aware of every movement—every tiny place his arm touched me on the back of my chair.

I don't respond to him beyond an irritated grunt before pulling the hotel key out of my bra and opening the door.

Whatever you say, Princess.

Jesus fucking Christ.

"So, what? Now that you're done playing pretend, you're just going to ignore me?" Sawyer closes the door behind us with a click, and I throw my shoes on the chair in the corner, painfully aware of the current sleeping situation.

I cannot share a bed with him.

"We never ordered a cot."

I can hear my heart beating. There is no way I'm going to make it through this. Since Sawyer has conveniently paid for everything so far—another fact that has my emotions all mixed up, maybe I can just get another room.

I can't. This hotel costs a fortune.

"It's fine," he says. "We can just share the bed."

"No!" My voice comes out too loud and strained. I blink a few times and try to clear my head. "No. I can sleep on the floor. It's fine."

"Georgia, that's ridiculous."

"I'm not sleeping with you, Sawyer." I'm pretty sure my voice goes up an octave at the end. Way to play it cool.

"Wow." He holds his hands up. "It's not like I was asking you to have sex with me. Relax." He unbuttons his shirt, and I have to force myself to look away. My cheeks are on fire.

I knew Sawyer was attractive. I've known that all along. But he has also been a complete and utter asshole. I really think the coffee, the cab, the sandwich, his words—it's all messing with my mind right now. Maybe I'm going insane.

I'm definitely going insane.

Sawyer speaks again, and I close my eyes, desperately trying not to hear his voice in my head when he said all those things earlier. *Make you squirm a little?*

No luck. The memory is loud and clear but drowned out by whatever he's saying now.

"It won't be an issue. They gave us a million pillows. We can just shove them down the middle and make a wall. You won't even know I'm here."

I don't want to sleep with Sawyer.

I don't want to sleep on the floor for ten days.

I don't want to be an asshole and make *him* sleep on the floor for ten days. This was his trip, after all.

"Fine," I say, giving in. "We can make a barrier. I'm going to get changed."

I grab my clothes from my suitcase and walk into the bathroom, immediately splashing cold water on my face before taking my makeup off, peeling the contacts out of my eyes, and getting ready for the longest night in history.

The bathroom in the hotel is nice, but it took me

forever to figure out how to flush the toilet. There's a button on the wall next to it. When we were here earlier, I thought for sure I would have to ask for Sawyer's help. At least I hadn't taken a shit.

When I finally walk out in my t-shirt and sleep shorts, tying my hair into a bun atop my head, Sawyer is leaning over the mattress in a pair of black sweatpants and no shirt. He's strategically placing pillows down the center of the bed to split it in two.

Thank God.

I don't think there's a barrier wide enough at this point. I can already feel the way my stomach is twisting, the flush working over my skin. My eyes catch his toned chest and the dusting of hair on his stomach leading down to the—

Fucking hell, Georgia! Are you this touch starved?

Sawyer doesn't say anything, and I don't mention the fact that he's shirtless. Usually, I'd say something sarcastic about his state of undress, but I firmly believe I have lost any and all ability to function.

He is smiling at me when he sidesteps to go to the bathroom, his toothpaste and brush in hand. I don't miss the way his arm brushes against mine.

Crawling into bed as quickly as possible, I close my eyes and hope that the peaceful calm of sleep will wash over me and I won't be left thinking about the way I had to squeeze my thighs together while he whispered in my ear.

What would Emerson say if she knew I was attracted to her brother?

She probably wouldn't care, except for the fact that I've spent so much time hating him, she would be utterly confused.

Hell. I'm confused.

"It's just physical," I whisper to myself, squeezing my eyes shut and waiting for the exhaustion to settle in.

"What is?" Sawyer asks, already done in the bathroom, walking over to his suitcase to tidy up by shoving everything inside.

"What is what?" Now I'm embarrassed. This is the worst trip in the existence of all trips ever. Maybe if I kill him, I can kill all these strange emotions with it—bury them six feet in the earth where they belong. That's where they can rot and wither—possibly rise again as a zombie. Are zombies stronger than alive people? Would killing off my emotions make them thirstier?

I *cannot* afford to be thirstier.

"Physical? Is that what you just said?" He doesn't seem like he thinks anything beyond the fact that I'm being incredibly weird, and I'm thankful for that.

Trust me. They won't question it.

"Grading," I offer. "The grading I brought. I was trying to gas myself up to complete it."

The lie tastes bitter on my tongue, and it isn't believable either, but Sawyer accepts it.

He laughs, crawling in on the other side of the bed. I can feel the way the mattress shifts, and I squeeze my eyes shut, but the backs of my eyelids project a very intriguing image where Sawyer is undressed—possibly sweaty. He's way too close. Especially if my mind is currently crafting pornographic images of the man against my will. "I think correcting papers is more mental, Georgia. But I'm no expert."

"Right."

I can already tell that my lengthy nap has ruined my sleep. I'm going to be up for a while and tortured by my own personal movie theater. The director being my indecent thoughts, and trust me, she's *filthy*.

Fantastic.

"I'm not really tired," Sawyer interrupts. "I think my sleep schedule is off after the plane ride. Do you want to watch something on the television?"

Maybe watching something mindless will help me relax enough to fall asleep. Maybe I won't be so distracted by the image of shirtless Sawyer burning into my brain. He looks good. Really good.

"Sure," I say, turning to prop my one remaining pillow up so I'm not lying flat on my back. I fluff it up a little and lean against the headboard.

Sawyer flips on the television, and we settle on watching some French soap opera that is objectively bad.

It doesn't even have subtitles, so we only understand half of it. Luckily for me, I know more than Sawyer, so I can answer some of his questions as the episode plays out. That brings me some satisfaction; however, the characters speak so fast I struggle to keep up with it all. Two years of French didn't help beyond the basics, and they didn't teach us any of the fun stuff either.

Like how to insult people.

After a few episodes, and silence from Sawyer's side of the bed, I finally start to feel the weight of the day and adjust my pillow to lie down.

With our formidable fortress separating us, I roll over, my back toward the pillow wall, and close my eyes as the television turns off.

"Hey, Georgia?" Sawyer says, and for the first time probably ever, my name on his lips doesn't sound like an insult.

"Yeah?" I say.

"Thanks for doing this. Pretending, I mean."

I'm surprised to hear him thanking me. It isn't often that Sawyer Owens says something overtly kind. He has done plenty, though—plenty to show that he isn't as much of an asshole as I thought.

I can't shake the thought that some of my reactions weren't pretending at all. The goosebumps I felt with his face so close to mine were real.

Very real.

I nestle myself further into the pillow as my breathing evens out, and I finally feel relaxed enough to think about sleep.

Sawyer hasn't said anything else, and I assume he's expecting me to ignore him. I don't, though.

"No problem, asshole," I say. "Thanks for the free trip."

I fall asleep to his soft chuckle, and the worst part of that is I don't actually hate the sound. Not at all.

I do, however, think I'm going to hate myself for the rest of my natural life.

THIRTEEN

Sawyer

When I wake up, the pillows are still firmly in place at the center of the bed, though I've noticed Georgia has one arm and one leg flung over the top.

I laugh to myself, slowly sliding off the mattress so I don't wake her.

She agreed to attend a cooking class with Warren and Sadie this morning, so I'll need to go find breakfast and make sure I'm ready in time to leave. We will have to call a cab, too.

After brushing my teeth, I throw on an undershirt, a vertical striped, short-sleeved button-down, and some khaki pants. My mind continues to circle back to the same phrase over and over again.

It's not exactly unbelievable that I'd find you attractive.

That one line is going to be the death of me. I thought Georgia would choose something else.

Strangulation, maybe? I didn't expect for this to be the way she'd have me go.

Walking out of the bathroom, I halt.

Georgia is standing at the foot of the bed in a pair of jeans and a bra. That's it. A bra and no shirt.

Her shirt is actually in her hands as she spins around and shrieks, lifting it up to cover her chest. It doesn't change the fact that I caught a glimpse of her black lace bra and the swell of her breasts and—

Oh shit.

"I can go back in the bathroom," I supply because I need to get out of this situation—fast.

"You were in there, and I thought—" She waves a hand. "It's fine. I'm sorry."

She lifts the shirt up, pulling it over her head and I hate myself for looking again—if only for the briefest moment.

I turn away and sit on the desk chair, dragging the booklet of *Things to do in Paris* over my lap to hide any evidence of how good Georgia Clark looks shirtless.

I'm not actually looking at anything in the book when Georgia gathers her toothbrush, toothpaste, and makeup out of her suitcase.

"I was just about to get breakfast," I say. "You could come if you want."

I sound like an awkward teenager. Granted, I'm only asking her to breakfast, but I did, in fact, ask immediately after seeing her shirtless. I'm also sitting here, in this chair, hiding a boner I shouldn't even have.

"We're spending an awful lot of time together," she

says, looking through her makeup bag. Her hair is down and still curly, hanging to her mid-back. "First breakfast, then a couple's cooking class."

A half smile pulls at my lips. Georgia really isn't that bad. "It's not so terrible," I respond. "I liked watching that show last night."

She's looking at me now, still holding all her things. "Me too."

For a moment, the air crackles between us, and I wonder if she's feeling some of this too. Maybe it's completely one-sided.

It's probably one-sided.

Georgia clears her throat before speaking again. "This class," she starts. "Do you know how much it's going to cost?" I can hear the trepidation in her voice and wonder how much she has to spend. I promised her a vacation, and now she's spending her money on activities that help support the lie I'm forcing her to tell. "I don't expect Sadie and Warren to pay for the cooking class, too."

Right.

The class is only a couple hundred dollars, and if I'm being honest, I had been saving up for this trip for a while. Originally, I was expecting to spend money on Anna, but if Georgia is willing to go to this thing, I don't mind paying for it. It's not like I don't have it.

"Don't worry about it," I say as I stand from the desk chair. "I'll take care of it."

Her eyes widen. "Sawyer, you can't do that. You've paid for literally everything so far."

I smile, winking at her as I say, "I had to repay you

for those feet pics you gave me. Wouldn't want to diminish their worth."

She lets out a strained laugh before I can see her usual sarcastic demeanor take over again. "For as much as you talk about feet—"

I honestly think she's questioning it.

Something about it has me cackling. A deep laugh that I can feel all the way to my abdominal muscles. "I don't have a foot fetish, Georgia." I'm practically crying at the insinuation. It was just too funny. I wipe my eyes before continuing. "Don't worry. I'm pretty standard in the bedroom."

I spin the desk chair around once, still fighting off the laughter.

"So, what you're saying," she starts. "Is that you talk a big game, thrust for two minutes, and then roll over?" My eyes snap to hers, seeing nothing but wicked humor behind her gaze. "I kind of feel bad for all the women you've dated. I feel bad for *myself*. Does Warren know how you treat me?"

I know she's joking, but I still can't get her words out of my mind. They're on repeat like a broken record.

It's not exactly unbelievable that I'd find you attractive.

Just to mess with her, or maybe to feel out whatever is happening between us, I allow myself to lower my gaze, trailing over her body and imagining what it might be like to see all of Georgia Clark. "That's not how it usually goes." My voice is low as my eyes meet hers, and I swear I can see her chest rising and falling more rapidly.

Her eyes are like fire, mouth parted as we stare at one another. I wonder if she can breathe. I know that I'm struggling.

Standing up from the chair, I turn when she surprises me with her next question.

"It's not?" she asks.

I raise an eyebrow. My entire body feels warm, and I shove my hands into my pockets. "Are you curious?"

Georgia sucks in a sharp breath before turning around to straighten the bed sheets. Her brows furrow, and just like that, we are out of whatever the fuck that was.

"No," she insists. "That's disgusting."

"You're the one that asked."

I walk over to her slowly, noting how she turns to face me. Her eyes glazed over with—something.

Her lips look soft, tinted pink. I can almost imagine what it would be like to feel them on my own. I don't stop those thoughts as I move to stand directly in front of her.

I'm looking down, and her breathing is definitely shallow. It fuels something inside me.

"You sure?" I'm looking at her now, and every nerve ending in my body must be misfiring. This is *Georgia Clark*. I can't stop it, though. After laughing with her over French soap operas last night, something settled within me. Maybe she's capable of more than just throwing barbs out. Maybe I could actually see myself liking her.

"Positive," she says, and she sounds a bit breathless.

I want to reach out and touch her, to run my fingers across her lips just to check if my theory is correct. I don't, though. I just stand there, allowing the tension to stretch between us.

"Will you be joining me for breakfast?" I finally ask.

"Yeah," she mutters, picking up her things and walking around me to the bathroom like she's trying to get away. She clears her throat. "We should probably go soon if we are going to make it to the cooking class in time."

"Just let me know when you're ready."

FOURTEEN

Georgia

After whatever that weird bedroom situation was, Sawyer and I went down to eat breakfast together. Over coffee and bread stuffed with chocolate, he asked me about my job.

I let myself talk.

And talk.

It isn't often that I find someone willing to let me rattle on about my students. It's hard because, usually, the person I'm talking to doesn't know the kids. That's why I save the school talk for Mrs. King.

Sawyer didn't say anything about me being annoying. He just let me go on about my student Miles and how interested he has become in ecology. I almost wonder if he will end up doing something with science in college. Something about that makes me immeasurably happy.

I'd love to say it's because it makes me feel like a

good teacher, but I can't lie about that. It's because whenever Miles talks to me about what he wants to do, his face lights up with excitement. Seeing students experience joy is one of the highlights of the job.

I was able to listen to Sawyer, too.

His job was nothing like what I thought it was. For one, I thought he was rich. He is, in fact, not. He also busts his ass. He told me all about the head chef Leo, and how he doesn't let Sawyer try out new recipes for the restaurant. It's really a shame because some of the things he described sounded to die for.

Despite being inferior in every way when it comes to culinary arts, I'm excited to have my chance to impress him at our cooking class.

When we get into the building, Sadie finds me right away and wraps me in a warm hug. I'm not usually one for physical contact between strangers, but I'm finding I don't mind it much with her.

"I'm glad you guys could make it," she says, pulling away from me. "I love Warren, and I'm excited to be married, but the destination wedding is kind of getting to me."

"Forgive me if I wasn't supposed to know, but Sawyer mentioned something about your mother making it stressful."

Sadie lets out a breathy laugh. "You have no idea. You'd think it was her wedding." Her shoulders sag, and she rolls her eyes. "I was okay running off to the courthouse. The entire destination thing was her idea. I'm not entirely sure she didn't want a free trip to France funded by my father."

Something about that last phrase has my stomach churning uncomfortably. I try to smile, but I know it's strained.

"Anyway," Sadie starts, as if she doesn't notice.

Because she doesn't.

"I saw you and Sawyer at dinner the other night." She waggles her brows. "I'm sure I know how that night ended. He was all over you there for a second."

Well, this conversation took a turn for the awkward. If only she knew how we actually spent our night—watching a soap opera we didn't understand with a giant pillow fort to separate us.

"We didn't," I say, but when I think about it, it's probably wrong. If the image we were portraying was real, we probably would have. I'm failing already and we haven't even been here for five minutes.

Maybe my mother was right about my acting abilities.

I go for something true. "I thought he wasn't going to let me out of the hotel this morning, though. Thank goodness he was only taking me to breakfast."

I test out a casual laugh, but I can still feel the warmth radiating off of Sawyer as he stared down at me, saying all the right things to get me questioning exactly what would go on in the bedroom with him.

My face heats as my smile drops.

"I don't recommend the balcony," Sadie supplies at a whisper. "People *do* walk the streets late into the night."

I laugh then—genuinely.

"I hope you don't know that by experience."

She cringes, and the secondhand embarrassment

washes over me. I would have been mortified if I was caught doing that on the balcony of a hotel.

Sawyer walks over, taking my hand as if it's the most natural thing in the world. The contact is unexpected, but I lean into him, knowing that he's just putting on a show for his friends. His hands are warm, and something about the simple touch has my brain frazzled. I hate how much his proximity affects my body.

"All paid for," he says, smiling down at me. "We should be good to go."

An older gentleman with a gray mustache and fancy chef's hat walks to the front room, speaking with a thick accent. He asks us to follow him to the kitchen, and Sawyer drags me along, keeping his fingers locked with mine.

"You don't have to hold my hand. I think they get it." I whisper.

"Anxious to get rid of me?" He raises one eyebrow, and something about the way the corner of his mouth turns up has my stomach doing a flip.

I clear my throat. "No, I just don't know how much of this," I lift our locked hands for emphasis, "is needed. I don't think they're doubting us."

"Of course." He lets go of my hand, and my brows furrow. I don't like the emptiness I feel without him close.

We stand behind a counter, facing the front of the room where the chef is explaining what we are about to make. Four cooking stations line the large room, separate from the demonstration kitchen where the head chef begins almost immediately. It reminds me of a home economics room, but with way more steel, more supplies set out to work with, and more difficulty understanding what the actual hell the instructor is saying.

Sadie and Warren are chatting by their station. Warren nods to me, saying something I don't catch. All I know is that we are about to make macarons and Sawyer is messing with his phone. He may cook for a living, but it's disrespectful to attend a cooking class and neglect to pay attention. Plus, I don't know what I'm doing, and the instructor is moving so quickly. I'm afraid I'll miss something.

I swat Sawyer's arm.

"Put that away," I hiss.

Sadie and Warren are still staring at us, and the chef, whose name is Guillaume, lets us know we will be separating the eggs from the egg whites.

Something I have literally never done in my life.

Sawyer slides his phone into his pocket and finds the eggs set out on the counter. I snatch one from his hand, somewhat irritated by his behavior.

"You didn't even pay attention. I'll do it." The smug smirk on his face brings up feelings that have been dormant since our strange dinner with his friends. I let them wash over me, and feed into the frustration.

Cracking the eggs, I try to separate the egg yolk from the egg whites with a fork and a spoon. I hear water running behind me, and then Sawyer is at my back, pressing his chest to me.

I think I stop breathing.

"You're right," he says. "They're looking at us." I can feel his breath on my neck, and I'm suddenly wishing I hadn't pulled my hair up. I'm certain he can see the goosebumps on my skin. Reaching around, he moves my hands to set down the spoon and fork and gently picks the yolk up with his fingers, separating it easily.

"Did you even wash your hands?" My nose wrinkles, and I try to hold on to the feeling of frustration—if only to keep my body's reactions at bay.

"Why do you think the water was running?" He's standing next to me now, grabbing another egg. "Though you should probably wash yours. Wouldn't want you contaminating our macarons."

I stomp over to the sink, using the soap while Sawyer continues working. Guillaume is quickly moving onto the next step, and I turn to see him explain putting almond flour into the food processor and sifting out the clumps.

I go to grab the sifter, but Sawyer reaches it before me, so I roll my eyes.

"You're infuriating. Let me do something." I sound insufferable, but right now, it's better than thinking of how warm his body was against my back, or how it felt to have his hands touch my skin. It's better than thinking about the questions he posed this morning in our room.

Suddenly, my face is hot all over again.

"Here," he says, sliding the confectioner sugar over. "Weigh this. He said a hundred grams."

"Grams?" I question, a bit confused. "Why not cups? What's the metric unit for cups?"

Wow. I teach science. I know this answer.

My mind is jumbled.

Sawyer gives me a flat look as he sets the scale in

front of me.

"With that kind of sugar, you can pack it down or fluff it up, it changes the amount." He is really getting off on knowing this stuff. It grates on my nerves as I use the small bowl and figure out how to zero out the scale.

"You know, I could probably just google that information." I'm focused on my task, trying to get the amount perfect. "You're not brighter just because you went to culinary school."

We spend the next ten minutes learning about mixing the dry ingredients together and then moving on the make the meringue.

That's when things turn south.

Listening to the instructor wouldn't be a problem if everything he was saying didn't sound like a dirty joke.

"Did he just say *soft peaks*?" I'm fighting off the urge to laugh, and I see Sawyer crack a smile, too.

"You're being immature." Sawyer is trying to keep his face straight, but I know he's struggling.

When I look over at Sadie and Warren, Sadie is standing with her back against the counter, and Warren is caging her in, probably whispering something sweet into her.

"They're touching." I'm suddenly aware of how little we've interacted since the eggs. "Should we touch?"

Sawyer's brows raise, and his brown eyes lock on mine. "What?" he says. It's then that I see the wicked smirk pull at his mouth. "Are you asking me to touch your soft peaks?" He's checking our meringue, and it looks about right.

"Shut up," I say. "You're being an asshole. That's not

what I meant." I'm also noticing how neat Sawyer's side of the counter is and how my side of the counter is—not. "I don't want you anywhere near my soft peaks."

Liquid fire. That's all I feel as I think about all the ways I might not mind that at all.

If Sawyer knows, he doesn't let on. He's simply grabbing the blue food coloring from the options set out for us.

"No," I say, grabbing his wrist. I'm leaning over the counter, holding his hand away from our mixing bowl. "Green. They should be green."

He scoffs and rolls his eyes, prying my fingers from his flesh. "Blue."

"That's selfish, asshole."

"Fine." He leans down, his face dangerously close to mine. "We can mix the two, and you're also right." His eyes flick to my lips briefly, and I'm fairly certain my legs are jelly. "They are touching. We should probably do something."

Nerves are skating around my body like professionals in the Olympics. He's still leaning close, his eyes flicking between mine. I wonder what he's thinking. Is he going to kiss me?

"I'll help you pipe the meringue once we put it in the piping bag."

And just like that, he's focused on the bowl. My heart is racing in my chest, and I swallow—hard.

"Right," I say a bit breathlessly, and I curse myself for it. I clear my throat, trying to gather my thoughts. "That's a good idea."

It's not a good idea. As soon as Sawyer is at my back

again, I'm engulfed in the scent of lemongrass. I'm pretty sure it's the scent of the body wash in our hotel room, so there's really nothing special about it. Still, I can't help the way it's making me dizzy.

His hands are on mine, and he's pressing me into the counter. Thank God his pelvis is keeping a respectful distance, or I may just break apart right here.

"Not bad," he says, guiding my hands as I apply pressure to the bag. He's helping with the motions and working on forming the perfect quarter-sized circle—exactly like the instructor told us to.

"Thanks," I say. I should throw out something witty. I should say something else. Instead, I lean back into him, allowing his touch to get my heart racing faster.

By the time it's done and Sawyer is tapping the tray down to get the air bubbles out—so he told me—I am ridiculously turned on.

I literally hate myself all over again. It's just like this morning in the hotel room.

My eyes are tracking the way he licks his lips as he uses a wooden skewer to carefully pop any remaining bubbles in our macarons. He's wearing an apron. I mean, I am too, but it should be a turnoff. Somehow, I like it. I like everything about it. Especially as my eyes travel down to the image of his firm, and completely toned—

"Georgia?" My eyes snap up to meet his, and I know by the very look on his face that he knows what I was staring at. "You like the view?"

I clear my throat. "What?"

His eyes track down my body, and I swear I can feel

every place his gaze touches. It's burning like fire. I'm burning like fire. Did they turn the air off?

He chuckles, taking our tray to the instructor at the front before coming back with a new tray. Tiny cups stand next to one small spoon on top of the cookie sheet in Sawyer's hands.

"These are the different fillings," he says. "They're all pre-made, and we're supposed to pick one."

Sadie walks behind me with her own tray. "How's everything going?" she asks. "I feel like this instructor is all business. He doesn't chat much."

I offer a half smile. "I guess he's paid to teach us how to make these."

"I'm so excited to try the jam filling," she says. "It looks to die for!"

And just like that, she's gone—off in her own Warren bubble—leaving me with Sawyer and my lusty thoughts all over again.

Fucking hell.

I pick up the spoon, ignoring Sawyer Owens, and dip it into one of the jams.

Before it gets to my mouth, Sawyer is leaning against the counter and facing the opposite direction. He grabs my wrist, wrapping his lips around the spoon and eating the jam I had portioned for myself to try.

He's smiling down at me, and I'm trying not to fall apart so thoroughly. My eyes are wide, lips parted as I stare at him smirking.

He knows. He fucking knows.

"Delicious," he says, turning around to lean over the

counter. "Would you like to try some?"

"I—"

I'm never speechless. I always have something to say. In this situation, I've used my scientific knowledge to form the hypothesis that my mind is no longer working at full capacity. I'm sure of it.

Sawyer is holding out the spoon. The same spoon his mouth was just on.

God. Am I twelve? That shouldn't matter.

It does. It matters. Especially as I see the subtle shift when our eyes lock, and I drag his hand toward my mouth, licking the jam off the spoon without losing eye contact.

I think I'm going to faint.

I think he's going to faint.

He's standing closer now, his chest rising and falling, his body warm. I don't dare look down. Not while his soft lips are still parted and his eyes are so heated.

"Do you want to be really convincing?" He's speaking low. "Give them a real show?"

I nod, not really thinking about Sadie and Warren at all.

Slowly—too slowly—Sawyer places his finger under my chin, running his thumb over the corner of my mouth. He looks at the jam on his finger before making eye contact. His brown eyes are blazing, and I am fighting for oxygen. I can feel the warmth wash over me as he flicks his tongue over the pad of his finger and sucks the jam off his flesh.

I need to touch him.

He takes a step closer, and my senses are out of control. Leaning in, I can almost feel the tension like a lightning storm.

"Georgia," he whispers. "I'm going to kiss you now."

"Okay." There's nothing I want more, in this moment, than to kiss Sawyer Owens. I am not thinking about Sadie or Warren. I'm not thinking about our instructor. All I can seem to think about is the dampness between my thighs and the way his lips look.

"Are you ready?" he asks.

No. "Yes,"

He leans in, his lips covering mine, and I don't know that I've experienced anything like it. Every cell in my body is on alert as his hand grips my waist, dragging me closer. His other hand shoves into my hair as he deepens the kiss, and I can feel him—hard as a rock against my stomach.

Oh god. Oh my god. Good God. Jesus Christ.

I'm pretty sure Sandra Owens would scold me for how many times I just used the Lord's name in vain. I can't really bring myself to care. Not as his tongue trails along my lower lip, and not as a small noise escapes me, betraying any façade that this was not real.

Is this real?

Do you want to be really convincing? Give them a real show?

I'm convinced.

My hands are trying to drag him closer by the apron as if *closer* was even possible.

"Get a room!" Warren's voice has us breaking apart. My cheeks are on fire, and I can't tell if it's from embarrassment or the kiss.

Sawyer is breathing heavily, but so am I.

He offers me a crooked smile, turning around to say

something to Warren. My ears don't even register it.

I'm pretty sure my entire world just imploded.

I want Sawyer Owens.

I want him so badly that I can't even remember a time I didn't want him. So badly that I don't know how I'm going to make it through tomorrow, pretending like that didn't just happen. It wasn't fake—not all of it could have been fake. It definitely turned him on because I could feel his—

"So," he says, leaning his elbows on the counter and looking down at me.

"So." My voice is nearly a whisper.

"The jam was pretty good, right?"

I can't help but think he's asking me a different question—one loaded with all sorts of things I'm going to have to unpack.

"Yep," I say, nodding and refusing to look at him anymore. He's almost painfully beautiful. "I say we choose the jam."

FIFTEEN

Sawyer

She finally did it.

She killed me.

With that one mind-melting kiss, Georgia Clark accomplished exactly what she set out to do. She sent me to my grave.

It was a good way to go.

Walking down the sidewalk near our hotel, Georgia and I don't speak. I'm not really sure what to say after that. On one hand, she definitely felt it. She *had* to feel it.

On the other hand, just because her body responded a certain way to me doesn't mean things have changed. My mind is a mess, and I'm trying to decode exactly what the fuck is happening.

"So," Georgia starts. She's keeping her distance from me, and it has me questioning how much of what she did was an act. "I was thinking about getting lunch. Do you want to come?"

I need to say something. More importantly, I need to understand what just happened between us, but I don't want to make assumptions and scare her off, so I go with the most reasonable option—the safest option. I point out the obvious.

"But Sadie and Warren aren't here." As the words leave my lips, Georgia's face twists into a scowl. She's staring at the sidewalk, and now I'm afraid because scowling Georgia is absolutely terrifying.

I'm also afraid of reading this the wrong way—of thinking that she is warming up to me—how I've warmed up to her. She *did* just ask me to get lunch with her, but the way she said it could have meant anything. She could have been asking out of obligation.

"Yeah," she huffs a laugh. "Forget I asked."

She wants me to go with her. This is it. There had to be a part of her that wanted it, too. I can still taste her lips on mine, feel the way her body pressed into me, the way she dragged me closer by the apron I was wearing.

I want to do that again so bad it hurts.

"I can." We are still walking, and the entrance to our hotel is approaching quickly. "Get lunch with you, I mean." I'm suddenly nervous, feeling like a fumbling teenager who is trying to ask a girl out. She has destroyed me in every way possible, and in the back of my head, I realize that she may have done it through pretending. "If you want me to," I add, just to be safe.

"No."

Ouch.

She straightens as she walks, lifting her head. "That's unnecessary. I just figured I'd ask."

Just figured I'd ask. My chest tightens as doubt creeps in like a thief in the night—a thief set on destroying any and all hope.

Before I respond, I laugh a little to sound casual. I can't stop running my hands through my hair. "I'm surprised you're not insulting me right now." The kiss was my idea, and that thought brings about other worries. "After what I made you do in there, I thought for sure you'd be shoving me off the Eiffel Tower. Sadie and Warren were convinced, though."

She winces as if I've said something hurtful.

"La Tour Eiffel," she corrects. "And if you'd like me to insult you, I'd be more than happy to."

I stop walking, turning to face her as a group of teenagers speaking French pass us on the sidewalk. They don't even look at us, just continue toward the endless number of lampposts lining the street. I watch them go, waiting for . . . something.

Georgia turns to look at me, her eyes blazing like fire. I can't read what she's thinking, and it's irritating me—grating on my nerves because all I can seem to think about is kissing her again. I want to lean in and test the waters. My eyes flick to her lips, pressed together in a thin line. She's pissed at something, and I can't seem to figure out what it is.

"Would you like me to insult you?" she asks.

I don't say anything. I can't say anything because I'm not exactly sure I know what *to* say. *That was the best kiss of my entire life, and I'm thinking I would like to do it again* seems too

124

forward. She's offering to insult me, and deep down, I would give anything for her to tear me apart with her words. If only she would put me out of my misery.

Something shifts in her demeanor, and I can't tell if it's still just anger or disappointment. Maybe I should just come out and tell her I enjoyed spending time with her. I liked going to breakfast with her and watching that ridiculous soap opera. I had fun making macarons and would do it again in a heartbeat. Even if she made fun of me for being a know-it-all the entire time. Especially then.

I open my mouth to say something before she cuts me off.

"You're an asshole," she says. I reel back, schooling my features to hide my shock as she leans in with the force of her words. "You're cocky and arrogant, and you were entirely too full of yourself in that kitchen." She raises a brow. "Do girls usually swoon when you flaunt your cooking knowledge? Because I wasn't really impressed."

Damn.

I have no idea what I did to set her off, but we are suddenly back to insult ping-pong. She's bubbling over with rage, and I can't imagine what I did to deserve everything she just tossed out at me. It stings, and something about that has me on edge, ready to fire my next shot and call her out on her bullshit.

I don't hold back. "You seemed pretty impressed," I say, remembering the noise she made when I traced her bottom lip with my tongue. *She's lying.*

"Then you read me wrong."

I halt.

Then you read me wrong.

Maybe I did read her wrong. She is getting a free trip out of this deal, and I asked her to pretend to be my girlfriend in exchange. She's doing me a favor.

"I'm going to get lunch," she says. "I'll take some time to tour the city."

Georgia is already walking off, and I can see the tension through her shoulders. She is practically running away from me, and my head is a mess of all the things I could have done to ruin whatever was happening.

Then you read me wrong.

I can't help the incessant thought echoing through my mind, telling me I did, in fact, read her wrong. Nothing is happening between me and Georgia Clark. Maybe she's upset that I made her kiss me at all. I asked her to, but in that situation, she didn't really have an option, not if Sadie and Warren were watching.

"Don't wait up," she tosses over her shoulder before leaving me standing on the sidewalk in front of our hotel— more confused than ever.

"Fuck," I mutter, not sure if I should follow her or just leave her alone.

I opt for leaving her alone. If I truly read her wrong, chasing her down would prove her point entirely. It would make me an asshole. An asshole that forced her to kiss him.

~

After pacing the hotel room, consumed by my own thoughts, I decide to spend the trip the way I originally planned.

Separate from Georgia and enjoying Paris.

Alone.

I put the small bag of macarons in the fridge and settle on going to the Eiffel Tower. Maybe I'll run into her, and she can shove me off the top like she so clearly wants to.

I get a cab even though the tower isn't far from our hotel. The blue sky stretches over the massive structure, and I notice how busy it is. Hundreds of tourists wait in line beneath the tower for their chance to climb to the top.

After paying, I decide to take the stairs instead of the elevator, hoping it'll be a good way to blow off some steam.

It is. By the time I get where I'm going, my legs are on fire, my thoughts gloriously empty. It's only when I look out at the city stretched below that the thoughts creep back in.

The wind whips around me, and there are friends, and couples—families all taking pictures of each other at the top, documenting their once-in-a-lifetime experience.

I pull out my phone, thinking of asking someone to snap a picture. Instead, I text Georgia.

Me: Hey, you good?

It's the dumbest text message I've ever sent. I know it is. And to absolutely no one's surprise, I don't get a response.

I find a restaurant and take my time eating, sitting outside so I can watch people passing.

When I get back to the hotel, I decide to call

Emerson, mostly because I've spent hours alone, and it would be nice to talk to someone I can understand. I should probably take some French classes. With all the alone time I'm about to have on this trip, I could download an app and learn a few things.

"Bonjour!" Emerson's voice is too chipper as she answers, and I groan internally.

"That's the dumbest thing you've ever said."

"Mom told me to do it."

I'm leaning against the dresser in the hotel room, switching my phone to my other ear. "You're home?"

"Yeah, loser. Say hi."

I can hear my parents in the background, and I suddenly feel homesick. I won't admit that, though.

"So, how's France?" Emerson asks. "I assume you're having a wonderful, solitary vacation. I just got off the phone with Georgia."

"Yeah?" I say, dragging my phone down to check if I have any new messages. I don't.

"Yeah. She mentioned something about a cooking class and you being completely insufferable, but I heard she got to go inside that huge arch today. The one built by Napoleon."

"She's more insufferable than I am." My mind traces back to what happened on the sidewalk, and as I suspected, I still don't understand it.

"Look, Sawyer. I don't mean to be a Debbie downer, but you *are* pretty insufferable. I mean it in the most loving way."

"Oh, I'm sure." Something about the way she says it

has me smiling.

"I recommend chilling it on the fake-dating thing, though. Georgia said you were intense."

That has me pausing. "What else did she say?"

"Nothing really. She was just checking in. Aside from you being really intense about acting like her boyfriend in front of your friends, your generally unpleasant attitude, she just told me about all the cool shops she visited. I'm pretty sure I'm getting a scarf. Have you gotten me a gift yet?"

I chuckle. "No. I'll get you something."

"You better. Hey, I have to go. Mom is trying to start a family board game."

I switch my phone to my other ear again. "Of course she is. Tell everyone I love them."

"You got it."

"You too, Nemo."

I hear Emerson cackle right before the phone disconnects.

Then you read me wrong.

I did. Most definitely. I also hate myself for it.

The door clicks open, and as if my own thoughts summoned her, Georgia enters the room with bags on her arms. She doesn't acknowledge me, just walks past and throws them on the chair.

"Oh look, you're using your own money."

She pauses, her back to me as she faces the balcony. I can see that I've hit a nerve, and it ignites a fire in my veins. It feels good to hate her.

"I never asked you for money." Georgia turns around, clearly upset by my presence already.

"You *did* tell Emerson that I was insufferable and taking things too far."

She laughs—a hollow and vicious sound. "That's not breaking news, Sawyer. I'm surprised you're just now figuring it out."

I grind my teeth together, trying to get rid of the anger I feel. I don't know what I expected, but it wasn't Georgia coming back to spew venom or me doing the same.

"I thought maybe you were warming up to me." The words sound too vulnerable, and I clench my fists at my sides.

"What makes you say that?" Georgia is staring at me, standing three feet away with her head cocked to the side. She hasn't, once, brought up the kiss or what happened.

"You're terrible at communication," I toss out, my frustration rising.

"What the actual *hell*, Sawyer." She is now fuming.

"And I ate all the macarons," I add. It's a lie. They're still in the fridge, but I want to see how she's going to react.

Georgia grabs her clothes from her suitcase and her toiletries. She's ripping them out of the bag with the force of a wild storm.

When she turns, she's glaring at me. I'm pretty sure I see smoke coming out of her nostrils. I think she's just a few steps away from turning into a dragon.

"You're a child!" she yells, pushing past me and slamming the bathroom door.

"And you're—" *A liar.* I want to call her a liar, but I can't get the words to leave my tongue. Not because she isn't a liar, but because that is exactly what I asked her to do. I asked her to lie, and I asked her to do it well.

The door to the bathroom opens, and suddenly she's standing just outside, begging for more. "I'm what, exactly, Sawyer?"

Her hair is wild, her eyes wilder, greener, with the force of her anger. She's breathing heavily too, and I'm trying not to think about every ridiculous thought I've had about her body since she walked out of that same bathroom in her dress. I'm trying to sort through everything she's said to me.

I *liked* how it felt—having her talk to me. I enjoyed having her around, sharing about her life.

Something I didn't know about Georgia Clark is that once you get a taste of her approval, her kindness, you never want to let it go.

I haven't had one singular thought about Anna all day, and here Georgia is, standing and looking painfully beautiful with rage in her eyes. She's messing with my head.

I prowl over to her, looking down into her heated gaze. I swear for a moment, her breath catches, but I'm almost certain that I'm reading her wrong. Of course, I would read her wrong. Everything about this morning was an act—all of it. I hate it. I hate her for making me hate it.

"I fucking hate you," I say.

Her eyes catch fire. "The feeling is mutual."

And just like that, she's slamming the bathroom door again, and I'm left listening to the sound of water running.

SIXTEEN

Georgia

A week ago, I would have agreed with the statement. A week ago, it *would* have been mutual, but as I stand in the bathroom waiting for the water in the shower to heat up, I can't help but wonder if it isn't mutual anymore.

The most dominant feeling is hurt.

But that's my fault.

I can't stop thinking about what he said after the cooking class—after the kiss that shattered my entire world.

But Sadie and Warren aren't here.

Of course. He made it abundantly clear that we were giving them a show, so why do I still feel like it was something more?

After what I made you do in there . . .

Sawyer didn't *make* me do anything, but he believes he did because it's all just pretend.

All of it.

"Damn it,"

I push away from the counter, leaving my reflection to peel off my clothes, hoping the hot water of the shower will chase away my thoughts.

All I did was ask him to eat lunch with me, and it felt like rejection. I didn't think there could be anything worse than spending my time with Sawyer Owens. I thought being forced to lie to his friends—pretend to be his girlfriend—was the worst imaginable fate. Hating and being hated, pretending none of it was true. I didn't realize that wanting him so badly while he lied his face off would be the thing to actually wound me.

When I'm done feeling sorry for myself, I change, brush my teeth, get ready for bed, and slip out of our hotel room to call my mom.

I spent a chunk of time talking to Emerson, but I neglected to hold up my end of the bargain with my parents.

I find my way to the lobby and sit down in one of the slightly uncomfortable chairs to pull out my phone and dial her number.

"Georgia Peach! How are you?" My mom's voice travels through the line, and I groan at the nickname.

"Mom, you know that nickname is the least creative thing you've come up with."

"And someday you're going to miss it," she says. "You know—when I'm dead." I can hear her shuffling around in the background. The screen door to my old house opens and closes, and I know she's on the back porch. "I've been waiting to hear about your trip, considering the circumstances."

"What circumstances?" I ask.

"Georgia." Her tone is scolding—as it should be. Pretending to date Sawyer was my worst idea to date.

"Okay. It's fine." I'm lying to my teeth.

She sighs, and I know she isn't buying whatever I'm selling. "Is he being kind to you?"

The kiss felt incredibly kind. The kindest thing anyone has done for me. Too bad he didn't mean it.

"He paid for the cab," I offer. "And my sandwich. I *do* really like his friends, so it isn't all bad. I also wish you could be here. You'd love the city. I got to walk around today."

I tell her about my tour around Paris and explain how the L'Arc de Triomphe is beautiful. As I am telling her about its view that's to die for, I see Sadie walk out of the elevator.

"Hey, Mom. I should probably go. One of Sawyer's friends is here."

"Okay. Don't forget to send me the pictures you took today!"

I smile. "Of course."

Hanging up the phone, I notice Sadie looking around the room for—something.

Her eyes are red—cheeks puffy, and I'm almost positive she's been crying.

When she sees me, she looks like she wants to turn around and run, but gives up, walking to sit in the chair across from me in the lobby.

"Hey, how are you?" I ask. I know her mother has been kind of obnoxious about the wedding, but earlier today, she seemed so happy. I wonder what could have changed so quickly.

Dumb question. Look at you and Sawyer.

I wince.

"This is embarrassing," she says by way of greeting. "But you already saw me." It's then that her face crumples, and I'm staring at a stranger—a crying stranger.

I have no idea what to do in this situation. I consider using one of the French magazines on the end table to pat her on the back, picturing myself saying *there, there. It'll all be okay.* The only problem is I don't know if it will be okay, and I don't really even know her.

This is fine, I tell myself. *You comfort your students all the time. Just be there and listen.*

I sit up, resting my elbows on my knees. "It's not embarrassing. You're about to get married." I try to smile reassuringly; not sure it's working. "I haven't done that yet, but I'm pretty sure it's stressful. Whatever you're feeling is probably justified."

"Oh god." She looks up at the ceiling, and I really hope she isn't going to cry again. "You don't even know me. First, I'm confessing to fucking on a balcony, and now I'm crying in a lobby with you. My mother has made me insane."

I laugh then, genuinely. "Mothers can do that."

"She's insufferable, really."

Here we go. Lend an ear. Just like with your students. You like Sadie, and maybe it'll get your mind off Sawyer.

Sadie offers a wan smile. "I'm pretty sure she thinks this is her wedding. I'm trying to fight for—something. I don't know, maybe I just want to feel a little in control." She leans back in her chair, closing her eyes. "I feel so out of control." She sighs and opens her eyes to look at me. "I'm sure of Warren, though. Mostly. I'm not sure he doesn't want a divorce already since I'm acting like a crazy person from all the stress."

"Well," I start. "The good news is he can't divorce you yet."

She looks at me and lets out a strained laugh. "Right, right. Of course."

"I'm really not so good at this—relationship advice. I try with my students, but it's out of my element." I figure honesty is the best way to go here. The last thing I want is her thinking I'm a terrible person. "I can say that I admire what you and Warren have. You look so in love."

The corners of her mouth turn up, and she opens her eyes, looking at me. "So do you and Sawyer."

Red alert. Please get me out of this lobby.

Sadie sighs, settling if only for a moment. "I'm getting married in four days."

"I know, and I hope you guys are serving alcohol. I plan on getting incredibly drunk. Embarrassingly so."

Sadie laughs and sits up, her brown eyes scrutinizing me. "You and Sawyer seem sure of each other."

It's my turn to laugh—cackle, I mean. "Oh, trust me, we don't know a damn thing. In fact, we are so very unsure of one another that most of the time, I think I hate him."

"That sounds pretty normal to me. What do you hate about him?"

This is not where I thought this was going. I honestly thought I was supposed to be *her* therapist, not the other way around.

Well, therapy is expensive. I might as well take the opportunity. Especially after shopping today.

"He's arrogant, a true jackass half of the time. He says whatever he's thinking, even if it's terrible."

Her face lights up. "Warren does that too. I'm constantly shushing him around other people because the man has no filter." She props her elbow on the arm of the chair, resting her head in her hand. "Okay, so you hate him. What do you like about him?"

Oof.

I don't want to think about all the reasons I've started warming up to Sawyer. I want to scream at him in our hotel room again, tell him all the ways he's the worst. Deep down, I know exactly where that is coming from. It's not that I really want those things. I'm just outrunning the pain of rejection here.

"He's generous," I offer. "One time, I bought him a beer, and he paid me way too much for it. We weren't even together then. In fact, we were very nearly the opposite. I think he did it because he knows I'm poor." I can't help but continue. "He labeled the payment as *feet pics,* which I was definitely mad at, but it was honestly pretty funny. He *is* funny."

And now I'm talking too much. I can think of more; could list out the way he listened to me over breakfast. I could tell her I secretly like arguing with him and that despite his deficiencies in social awareness and the things he says, he's actually a pretty nice guy.

Damn.

"Enough about Sawyer and me." I wave a hand. "I

really think you and Warren should spend time together—
alone. Get away from your family for a while. I mean, you
are in Paris."

Sadie glances up at the chandelier hanging overhead.
"That's a good idea. I've spent a lot of time with my mother,
and I'm pretty sure I need a break." Her eyes are on me, her
smile wide. "Maybe you and Sawyer should do the same."

I nod, not quite knowing how to respond to that.

"I really like you, Georgia." Sadie is standing up now,
getting ready to leave. "You let me sit with you after crying
and looking totally crazy." Her smile is softer. "I hope
Sawyer keeps you around."

Oh, awkward. Little does she know; we are planning a
prompt break-up upon our return to the states.

"I should get going." Sadie turns, making her way
back to the elevator and leaving me with my own thoughts.

When I get back to our room, Sawyer is alone,
scowling, and watching the same cheesy French soap opera
next to a wall of pillows. I try not to laugh at the image, but
a small sound leaks out, and he finally looks over at me.

I walk over to my side of the bed and crawl under
the covers. Silence is stretching between us, and I don't feel
as angry anymore. "I'm going to Versailles tomorrow," I
begin. "Maybe tour the castle. I hear they have bikes you can
rent to go through the gardens."

Sawyer nods, flipping off the television and adjusting
himself to lie down. "Have fun." His tone has a bite to it.

I can feel the hurt already, wishing it would go away.
The truth is, there are a lot of things I like about him, and I
really don't want to travel alone. Maybe if we had time with

one another—time without Sadie and Warren—I could figure out what is actually real and what isn't. Maybe if I'm brave—

"Do you want to go?"

I can hear the air conditioning blowing from the other side of the room, the only sound aside from the deafening silence.

"Why?" he asks.

I don't expect him to accept, not after earlier, but I decide to extend the olive branch, anyway. "I might like having you there," I confess.

He grunts from his side of the bed. "So, you can insult me."

A small smile tugs at my lips. "Maybe," I say. "Maybe I was just trying to lure you away so I can murder you in cold blood."

"Wouldn't surprise me."

I let out a chuckle at that. My thoughts about him have been murderous. The silence comes back even louder than before.

His voice cuts through. "I'll go with you, Georgia."

I hate the way my entire body lights up at those words—the way excitement skates through my body.

He continues, and I think I can hear him smiling as he talks. "Mostly because you're a twenty-something woman wandering France on her own, and I've seen the movie *Taken*."

"Awe," I say, sitting up so I can look at him over the great wall of pillows. He turns to gaze back at me. "That's kind of you to think about protecting your fake girlfriend."

It's then that I see his smile, and I'm pretty sure it's enough to knock me out. "Never know," he says. "I might try to murder you in cold blood, too."

I smile back, hoping he sees something besides malice in my expression. "Then may the best predator win."

I lie back down, feeling the bed vibrate as Sawyer releases a small chuckle.

I'm pretty sure he thinks I'm crazy. First, I'm kissing him, then I'm swinging insults at him like he's my enemy in a grand political race. Finally, I'm inviting him to tour a castle with me.

The last thought I remember having before I fall asleep is that this might be a terrible, horrible idea.

SEVENTEEN

Sawyer

I am emotionally constipated.

In the face of whatever feelings I have for Georgia, I decided the best course of action was to tell her I fucking hated her.

Which isn't true.

I mean, it was true before, but I don't hate her.

I'm not sure why I agreed to go to Versailles with her—especially after the shouting match we had, but something about the way she walked into the room, silent and pleading—I couldn't say no. Not when the opportunity to figure my shit out was handed to me on a silver platter.

Sadie and Warren won't be in the picture, and based on the number of times I've thought about the damn kiss, I need to sort out what is real and what isn't.

I drag myself off the bed, trying to keep from waking Georgia. She's sleeping on the other side of our great wall of pillows, breathing steadily.

I'm exhausted, but I can't sleep anymore. My mind is replaying the same scene over and over without relief.

The feeling is mutual.

I turn it over as I grab my clothes and head to the bathroom, wondering if it means she hates me or if she's thinking about the kiss, too.

Fucking hell.

I splash some cold water on my face and decide to head to the café near the hotel again. I could use breakfast and a coffee if I'm going to make it through this trip.

When I finally emerge from the bathroom, Georgia is sprawled out with her leg tossed over the pillows. I wonder if she knows I'm gone, or if, in her sleep—

Sawyer, stop.

Her hair is wild down her back, and my eyes linger on her for a moment. I shake my head, turning away before I become the creepiest asshole in all of history.

I need to get out of here.

The sidewalk is busier than I expected, and I dodge a group of teenagers laughing as they parade down the street. Pulling out my phone, I search for the number of a cab that can take us to Versailles. Making the phone call, I walk the rest of the way to the café.

Unfortunately, I couldn't understand half of what the man said on the other line. He explained the cost and the ticketing process, but his accent was so thick, I'm not sure if it will cost us thirty euros or a million.

He also started talking to someone in the background in French—which irritated me. If Georgia had been around, she could have made out a few words like she does with the soap opera we keep watching. Without her, I may have sold my identity to the French version of, *we are calling about your car's extended warranty.*

Great.

The café is decently busy, and I'm forced to wait in line. I don't have time to sit down, so I decide to grab some stuff for Georgia, too.

When I get to the counter, the accent nightmare continues. I think I say what about fifty times before I secure two mini breakfast quiches, a flat white for myself, and Georgia's ridiculous latte.

Walking back to the hotel, my mind goes back to the cooking class. I can see the way Georgia was looking me over, her hazel eyes lingering on my ass. That had to mean something, right?

Or she's a fantastic actress.

I shake off the spiraling thoughts, fumbling into the room with our breakfast and the hotel keycard. I kick the door open, spotting Georgia on the end of the bed, dressed in a form-fitting forest-green tank top and no—

Jesus Christ.

The tank is tucked into high-waisted jeans, and I'm fighting the urge to keep my eyes up—like a respectful gentleman. I refuse to notice the way she isn't wearing a bra. I straighten my stance and hold up the bag of quiches and the drinks.

"I figured you might like something other than chocolate-filled bread," I say. "You know. Since that's all the hotel seems to offer."

She glances at the bag in my hand and raises a brow, twirling a golden necklace between her fingers. The room is too hot. It's unbearably hot, and I can't stop thinking about the way it felt to have all of that pressed against all of me.

I need to sit down.

"I found something interesting in the fridge." Georgia is staring at me like I'm caught, and I can't help the spike of nerves that shoot through me.

"What's that?" I ask, trying to keep my tone steady.

"The macarons you said you ate."

That grabs my attention, and I let out a breathy laugh, hoping she doesn't see how much she's getting to me already. "I hope you didn't eat them," I say, smiling. "Whatever you found may have been filled with poison since I ate the ones we made."

Lie. Lie. Lie. You were behaving like a child when you told her you ate them.

Georgia gets up and walks from the edge of the bed until she is standing right in front of me. I keep the smile plastered to my face, knowing damn well I never ate the macarons. I was just trying to make her more upset—and it worked. Something about that fills me with satisfaction. I'm sure she can see it on my face.

"I had one," she admits, looking up at me with a challenge in her eyes. "I'm not dead yet."

I lean in just a hair, catching the wicked glint in her eyes. She still smells like pears, and I'm finding that I like the scent. Pears are a really fantastic fruit. "Give it time," I say.

Georgia grabs the bag of quiches out of my hand and her drink before her eyes narrow at me. "How do I know *you* didn't poison them?"

I risk looking--purely for scientific research. Surely someone who teaches the subject would understand. Yep. Definitely not wearing a bra. I peel my eyes away and swallow. My cheeks feel flushed, but I scan her face for any hint of—anything. I'm not really sure.

I want her.

I risk leaning in closer until I'm towering over her, but our faces are only inches apart. Her lips part and I can't get my head on straight.

Being this close to her has electricity skittering across my skin—lighting up every inch of me.

"I didn't poison it," I state. "If I were going to kill you, I wouldn't use poison." My eyes flick to her lips one more time, relishing in the way her breaths have become shallow. Maybe I didn't read her as wrong as I thought. "Anything I'd do with you would be done with my hands."

She's staring at me as the electricity intensifies, and I'm brought back to the last time we were this close, staring at each other while the world faded away. It was right before I told her I was going to kiss her.

Her eyes are blazing, becoming greener with whatever emotions she's feeling, and I'm held there, unable to break the spell.

Georgia does, though. She clears her throat and holds up the bag and her drink. "Thank you for the coffee." Her voice sounds a bit strained as she turns to walk away.

"Um, yeah." I follow her over to the armchairs by the balcony, finding my seat in the one next to her. "The cab should be here in twenty minutes," I offer. "I called earlier."

Georgia nods and hunches down, pulling her coffee close and taking a sip.

Deciding to drink my own, the silence stretches taut between us—filled with a million questions. I'm not sure what is real and what is fake, but considering we are alone, whatever just happened has to be real.

Right?

"You know," Georgia begins, breaking through my thoughts. "I'm not entirely sure how we started hating each other." She sighs, leaning her head back on the purple upholstery. "You may be an asshole, but you can also be thoughtful."

"Is that a compliment?" I can't help the way the corner of my mouth quirks up or the way my eyes slide to her. She's not looking at me. Maybe she's gone crazy. "Are you sure the macarons weren't poisoned?" I ask.

She cracks one of her eyes open, and I can feel her glare all over my body. It's like fire. "You tell me," she remarks.

I take another sip of my coffee, savoring the flavor of espresso. "I didn't touch them," I admit.

She is right about one thing; I can't remember when we started hating each other, either. I remember how she tossed my cookie in the trash, though, her eyes lighted with fire and determination—like they almost always are.

"I think it may have started with the cookie insult."

Georgia bursts upright. "I remember that! You told me to put my cookies in the trash, you asshat!"

I smile slightly. "Never said such a thing." I look out to the streets below, noting that the sidewalk is becoming more and more crowded. There's still no cab. "I said you could place them *by* the trash. Then you threw away one of the cookies I spent hours slaving over." My eyes slide to her. "You know, I had just finished a class learning how to make those. Absolutely brutal to insult me the way you did."

"Not as brutal as you were when you made fun of my job over dinner. In front of your *parents*." Georgia isn't looking at me. She leans down to open the bag and pulls out a quiche. "I've wanted to be a teacher for so long," she admits. "I think it became a part of who I am. I mean, I always felt like I was good at science, too." She leans back, taking a bite of the pastry. "I may be bad at gardening, but I care about the planet. You know, I originally wanted to be a conservationist or even an ecologist."

"You wanted to be a scientist?"

"I could have been if I wanted to." She's looking at me now, her eyes narrowed and her tone defensive.

"I wasn't saying you couldn't."

"You totally were." She pulls her knees up to her chest, resting her feet on the seat of the armchair. "See, this is why we hate each other."

I'm picturing her talking over breakfast, telling me about her students, and asking me questions about cooking. My heart is pounding steadily in my chest, a warm feeling washing over me. "Do we?" I ask, raising a brow.

"Well," she starts. "That's what you told me yesterday. I recall the words, *I fucking hate you.* If we're being precise." Her tone is dripping with venom, and I wince.

I really am emotionally constipated.

"I'm sorry about that." I let the pause settle between

us for a moment, trying to build up the courage to say what I'm going to say next. "I don't hate you, Georgia." I clear my throat, knowing I need to apologize to her. If what Emerson said is true—

"And about the kiss," I continue. "I'm sorry I did that. I shouldn't have forced you to go along with it." The thought of her thinking I was pressuring her to kiss me for this damn trip makes my stomach churn. "Emerson told me you confessed to me being too *intense*."

"You weren't."

It's quiet, and I'm trying to pick up on her meaning. "What?"

Georgia shrugs. "It wasn't the worst kiss I've ever had." Her eyes are closed again. I can't help rehashing every detail—the way she grabbed my apron. It certainly wasn't the worst kiss. Not in the fucking slightest.

"Who was the worst?" I ask her.

Georgia laughs a little, taking another sip of her coffee before answering. "Sebastian Thomas. I went on one date with him my freshman year. It was like kissing a brick wall."

I laugh at that. "My worst was with a girl named Ava. I was five, and I kissed her in a closet while standing on a giant mess of *Legos*."

Georgia sits up and swats at my chest. "Pretty scandalous for a first kiss!" she says, but there's no real accusation to her voice. "You were a harlot at five years old."

I can't take the smile off my face.

I watch outside the balcony as pigeons land on the roof across the street. "Okay," I say, trying to keep the conversation going. "Best kiss?"

It's silent—too silent. I look over to see her staring at me, an indecipherable expression on her face. "Georgia?"

"Oh," she says, somewhat flustered. "Right. Yeah. I guess I haven't really thought about that one." I swear there's a pink tint to her cheeks. "Your best?"

My brows furrow. That answer is easy. It's the very kiss I've been thinking about since Georgia Clark utterly destroyed me. It's the same kiss that's going to haunt my dreams, living on forever in my mind.

I can't tell her that, though.

Emotionally constipated.

I should eat some fiber.

I grab a quiche out of the bag. "Same," I offer, popping it into my mouth and chewing. When I swallow, I add, "I don't remember." The lie tastes bitter on my tongue, a direct contrast to the mini quiche I just ate.

"Well, that's pretty unfair to ask a question when you don't know the answer for yourself."

I take another sip of coffee to wash the food down as I see the cab pull up to the curb outside the hotel. My voice is low when I speak. "I guess so."

I can't help the sinking feeling that comes over me—like deep down I was hoping she would answer the question—like she would say the answer was ours.

EIGHTEEN

Georgia

The entire ride in the cab has me fidgeting in my seat, messing with the small rip in my jeans. I've never been so nervous in my life, and I'm not sure why.

You know why, Georgia.

It was easier when we were screaming at each other—easier before Sadie brought up all the ways I'm starting to like Sawyer Owens. None of those thoughts helped last night when I was trying to fall asleep, and they certainly aren't helping now.

The cab pulls up to the giant golden gates positioned in front of the largest building I've ever seen. Those nerves that were skating through my body keep on skating—like professionals.

It's unfortunate, really.

I glance back at Sawyer, who is jumping at the chance to pay for the car, and my eyes roll. I called him *generous*, and deep down I wish it weren't true. Maybe then it would be easier to fight off the fear of being rejected. I'm like a middle schooler with a hopeless, ridiculous, all-consuming crush.

I can't get rid of it.

It's infuriating.

All I know is I'm caught between wanting to fight and throwing myself at him like he's the king that built this insane castle—like I'm some poor peasant begging for his favor.

It makes me fucking sick.

Not as sick as the words rattling around in my skull. I didn't mean what I said, and I wish I could say he didn't mean what he said either.

I fucking hate you.

If it were true, he wouldn't be here.

Would he?

When I get out of the car, my cheeks are flushed, and I run my hands over my green tank to smooth out the fabric. It doesn't need it since it's obviously tucked in. I'm just nervous.

Like I said before.

"We had to order tickets online. I took care of it, but I'm not sure where we're supposed to go. The guy on the phone had a thick accent." Sawyer is rounding the car and adjusting the hood of his tawny-colored sweatshirt. He's wearing jeans that hug his—

Georgia, no.

I clear my throat. "We can just follow the crowds, I guess." I turn to offer him a small smile, and when he smiles back, my chest tightens painfully. He's beautiful.

I'm pathetic.

Just the other day, I was screaming at him in a hotel room and trying to let him know all the ways he's horrid, and I hate him. Then he asked me what my best kiss was, and I didn't have the guts to admit the truth. Somewhere between dinner and that damn cooking class, Sawyer has ruined me.

It feels like we are playing chess—swapping turns and throwing out cryptic messages about how attracted we are to one another. The only problem with that analogy is that I don't even know how to play chess. It seems incredibly boring, and all the pieces move in different ways. It's too much to remember.

Still, I'm stuck in a game with Sawyer, desperately trying to win. What am I winning? I wouldn't know.

We follow the crowd, hopping into the long line stretched from the palace doors. Thin gold paint and leafing covers much of the building. There are statues and intricate carvings everywhere, and I know my mother would be jealous that I'm here. I really should call her again. I miss my family a lot.

"Your eyes are as big as saucers." Sawyer's voice breaks my thoughts as he leans in. I can feel his arm brush against me before he leans away again. But with that small touch, he moved the first piece of the day. It's probably a pawn—you know, the small pieces—since the touch was so incredibly small.

Yet my body is on fire. I think I might burn in whatever hell Sawyer has created.

I love it.

My gaze snaps to his as the line slowly moves

forward. "There's so much to look at," I admit. "I can't even believe this place exists. It's huge." I look up at the windows lining the entire building. "This was someone's actual house."

"Ah," Sawyer says. "The very reason they started lobbing off heads with the guillotine."

I can't help but chuckle. He's funny. Why the fuck is he funny?

"Careful. I'm sure with your fancy sous chef salary your house is just as outrageous. I might have to lob your head off the moment I see it."

And just like that, I moved a chess piece of my own.

His brows pull together when I look back at him. "When you see my house?" He's speaking slowly.

Oh god. I knew I didn't know how to play this damn game. We are not really dating, and this isn't a real date. I'm not going to be invited to his *house*.

Alarm bells are blaring in my mind, and I need to fix this. I'm going to go the safe route. We are friends. Surely friends visit each other's houses.

"You know, since we are such close friends now, I'll see it when you invite me over for a game night." I'm scrambling here, but Sawyer doesn't seem to notice as he shoves his hands into his pockets. One side of his mouth quirks up, and relief washes over me. I swear he's the most beautiful creature I've seen. It's a shame, really—all the time I spent loathing him.

"I guess I'm hosting game nights at my *apartment*," he says as the line moves forward. "I already told you my salary isn't that big. What game should we play?"

Anything but chess.

I blurt out the first game that comes to mind. "Twister," I answer, and immediately want to die. *Rest in peace, Georgia.* I don't want to be here anymore. Why would I say that?

Sawyer's brows raise, and my cheeks flame. I feel out of control—like a complete and total mess. I backtrack, hoping that fancy chess tournaments come with an undo button where you decide to play differently. I'm pretty sure they don't, but I try anyway. "Or we could play Candyland. That one's a classic."

Honestly, Candyland is a horrible game. It's fun when you're a kid, but as you grow up, you realize it's painfully boring and was only fun because the illustrations were cool.

The line is really moving now, and Sawyer doesn't say anything until we are close to the doors. He leans in, whispering quietly. "I think I'd rather play Twister."

He's winning.

My stomach is flipping, and I suddenly feel like there's no oxygen. I don't dare look at him for fear of passing out.

That's definitely overdramatic, but I don't even care.

After making it through the line, we walk into the building and move toward the royal chapel. It's closed off, so you can only look out over a railing. I lean to get a better view and feel Sawyer move next to me. I'm trying to focus on the breathtaking artwork, but my mind keeps circling back to how close he is and the heat radiating off his body.

"Someone actually painted all of that on the ceiling,"

I say. I sound stupid, so I focus on looking out at the room. Tall pillars line either side of the chapel, and the rounded ceiling is painted between the golden accents above.

That's when it happens.

His next move.

As we move away from the chapel, I feel Sawyer's hand brush mine. I don't dare say anything. When our fingers touch, I don't look at him either. I'm afraid that if I acknowledge it, he's going to stop playing.

Please don't stop.

We walk through the rest of the palace, observing the rooms filled with finery. There are golden suns above every doorway to depict *the sun king*. Apparently, King Louis the whatever number called himself that and put the symbol all throughout the castle.

I'm surprised I'm even learning anything on this trip.

We pass under one of those golden suns as we move to the infamous *Hall of Mirrors*. Sawyer has been holding my hand on and off. It feels natural, but at the same time, a zap of electricity shoots through my skin every time he does it.

I really am a sad middle school girl with a crush— worse than my high school students.

I look up at the golden symbol again and let go of Sawyer's hand. "Kind of arrogant to create an image for yourself and plaster it around your entire palace," I remark.

"Isn't that what old moms do?"

I laugh, my brows creasing. "What?"

Sawyer is walking next to me, his hands in the pockets of his jeans. "Moms pick an animal they get attached to, and then start buying shit for their house that fits the theme." He gets ahead of me, turning around and walking backward with a smile on his face. The *Hall of Mirrors* is before us, but all I can do is look at him. "I don't know if you noticed this, Georgia, but Sandra Owens picked pugs. Next time she offers you a cup of coffee, take it. There will probably be a pug on it."

I've been to Emerson's parents' house a few times, and the funny thing is that Sawyer isn't lying. As I think about it more, I realize how true it is. They got a pug last year named Captain Hook, and Sandra does have a pug-themed bathroom.

My mother isn't immune to the theory, either. "Oh my god," I say. "My mother decorates with giraffes."

"What did I tell you?" Sawyer's smile is smug as he turns around again and stops in the center of the room, gazing at the large windows lining the wall.

"So, Georgia." He turns, planting himself in front of me. "What will it be? What animal speaks to you?"

I literally do not know how to answer that question. "I can say I've never been inclined to decorate my house with animals before."

"Oh, come on," Sawyer says, his brown eyes lighted as he stares down at me. "If you had to choose."

I smile, folding my arms across my chest in defiance. "Fine," I say. "I wouldn't choose. Just to spite you, I'll get a new animal every time."

"The spite thing is very on brand for you."

I lean forward, tilting my head further to look up at him. He held my hand, and I guess it's my move now. "You like it."

His mouth hangs open, and I can't help but think about how his lips felt on mine or how it felt to drag him closer. He stares at me for a second, and I expect him to toss something back, but instead, Sawyer pulls out his phone.

"We should take a picture. I haven't taken much, and I'd like to document the trip."

He moves to stand behind me, positioning his phone in front of us. I don't want to ruin the moment by bringing up Anna or his request that we don't take pictures, so I smile.

I can feel him leaning in, his chest brushing against my back. He smells like lemongrass again, and something about it makes my knees weak. Just before he takes the picture, he whispers, "You're also right. I do like it."

Oh god.

When I turn around, he's already messing with his phone and refusing to look at me. I probably look like a fish—my mouth hanging open, closing, opening again. I don't even know how to respond to him.

"There," he says, satisfied. He shows me his new lock screen with the photo he just took of us. We look— good.

I'm seriously a middle schooler.

"Okay, fine." I'm barely containing myself here, trying to think of my next move in our little game. "I want one for my background, too." I position myself in front of him again and grab my phone from my back pocket. Sawyer is smiling when I turn the camera to face us, and I can see the *Hall of Mirrors* in the background of the shot.

Just before I snap the photo, I'm pretty sure the earth stops spinning as Sawyer turns his head to plant a kiss on my cheek. My mind reels, and fire shoots through my blood as I stare at the screen. I really look like a fish now with my mouth open.

Maybe that will be my decorative pet of choice.

He's definitely winning chess.

"That'll be a good one," he says, gesturing to the phone before walking down the rest of the hall as if nothing happened.

I quickly set the picture as my lock screen and chase after him. I need to make sure that was real. It doesn't feel real.

"Why did you do that?" I ask. "Sadie and Warren aren't here."

He's still walking and refusing to look at me. "I think we should head to the gardens," he says as I fight to keep up with his large strides. My phone is in my hand, and my heart is still pounding in my chest.

He didn't answer the question, and I'm tired of trying to figure out what is really happening between us. I need to know what is really happening.

"Why did you do that?" I ask again.

Sawyer spins, towering over me as his brown eyes bore into mine. Satisfaction written on his face as if he is proud that he got me off balance with the kiss.

Lemongrass fills my lungs again, and I have to take a deep breath. It's like there's a thread between us, stretched so taut by the tension that it'll snap at any moment. I can almost hear my heartbeat as I wait for his response.

"Maybe I just wanted to," he finally answers.

Checkmate.

I suck in a harsh breath, watching as his eyes trail over my face, my torso, and back up. He smirks, turning around and heading to the gardens.

I'm offered no more explanation. Maybe he didn't win.

I follow him and note how immaculate the gardens are—manicured to perfection. There are fountains and flowers and a long gravel path that circles through plants I don't really care to identify.

My cheek is tingling where Sawyer kissed me, and I bring my hand up to touch the spot.

Maybe I just wanted to.

I'm definitely off balance.

"Imagine how expensive it would be to maintain this." It's lame. I know it's lame, but I am not thinking straight. "They'd have to hire people."

What am I saying?

"Well, they certainly wouldn't hire you," Sawyer says through a laugh.

I try to act normal, leaning into him as he walks next to me. "Rude." I can't help the small chuckle that escapes my lips—lips that are currently thinking about doing something else. "You're probably right. These people were so—"

"Rich?" he finishes, his eyes sliding to me.

"I was going to say pompous." I turn back, looking at the back of the castle. It reminds me of Mr. Darcy's house—just way more massive. I bet King Louis had a million carriages. "Still," I continue. "Doesn't this place make you want to watch *Pride and Prejudice*?"

"You know that doesn't take place in France, right?"

I turn around and notice that Sawyer feels proud of himself for knowing that. It's written all over his face as we walk down a set of stairs leading to the rest of the gardens. People litter the lawn, and tourists take photos of the flowers along the gravel trail.

This guy definitely had more carriages than Mr. Darcy.

"You've seen it, then?" I ask.

Sawyer's hands are in his pockets again. "Once in a high school English class." He cocks an eyebrow. "I fell asleep."

"Well, then we are going to watch that movie instead of the French soap opera. Say goodbye to Francois and Lillian."

He chuckles, turning around to face me and walk backward. "Are those even the names of the main characters?"

They aren't. I'm not sure I even understand what is happening in that damn show. My high school teachers would be so disappointed. "Yeah, I have no clue," I admit.

I still haven't made my move yet as Sawyer stops walking. He's facing me—looking down in a way that has that thread between us fraying. I want so badly to touch him—to relive whatever kiss happened during the cooking class. Only this time, I would know it was real.

My heart is pounding in my chest as he looks down at me. It's like he's waiting to figure out what I'm going to do next.

"I lied," I say, trying to summon as much courage as possible. Maybe my future house animal will be a lion. I can force all my children to watch *Narnia* repeatedly just to see Aslan on the screen. "I know what my best kiss was."

"Oh?" he says. I can see the slight crease between his brows—the one that lets me know he didn't expect the remark. He's also not going to expect the answer, either.

I lean in, waiting for him to pull away—to say something—anything. Sawyer doesn't. He just waits there, too, his eyes darkening and flicking to my lips briefly. I can feel that gaze like a brand.

His lips are parted, and I want him so badly I'm certain it's going to kill me. "It was ours," I finally answer.

He kisses me before I have a chance to move towards him myself. I can't think. All I know is that he's pushing closer, dragging me forward before his hands settle on my waist.

It feels just like the first time, and I whimper when his tongue traces the seam of my lips.

In this moment, we are the only two human beings on the planet.

Sawyer groans and I tangle my hands into his hair, trying to pull him closer.

I need more—more of him like this—funny and kind; all the things I didn't think he could be—the things I never knew I wanted.

He pulls back, keeping his forehead on mine as my heart thrashes against my rib cage. My lungs beg for more oxygen.

"There are people here," he says, his breathing just as ragged as mine. I don't want to admit what that does to me.

"Right," I say. "We didn't even get to ride the bikes." My voice sounds breathless.

Sawyer's chuckle rumbles, and I can feel every vibration move across my skin. It's doing all sorts of things to my body. "We can rent some bikes, Georgia," he says. "Then we can get some food. I'm starving."

"Okay."

I'm not really sure what's happening. First, we are kissing, and now he's talking about food.

"Do you want to get a late lunch with me?" he asks.

I pull back, looking into his eyes for any hint of his intentions. "Is this like a date?" I ask.

"Like a date," he answers, a smile breaking through. "A real one."

I stand on my toes, kissing the corner of his mouth before lowering back down.

I'm not sure who won whatever game we were playing. All I know is that there's no way I lost—not when Sawyer is looking at me and waiting for my response. Not when his hands are still on my waist, burning a hole through the fabric of my shirt.

"Sure, Sawyer Owens," I finally say. "I'll go on a date with you."

NINETEEN

Sawyer

I will never recover.

It was ours.

I've played the moment over repeatedly in my mind. I don't know what I did to win the lottery, aside from lying through my teeth and telling her I fucking hated her.

The longer I spent touring Versailles with her, the more I realize I can't even remember a time when I did hate her.

I might have memory loss.

We rode bikes around the palace gardens, taking pictures and laughing about how unsteady I was. There's some truth to never forgetting how to ride a bike, but it had still been a while, and Georgia was relentless.

As soon as we get in the cab, she pulls up a nearby restaurant on her phone and shoves it in my face. I can't even register what's pictured on the screen before she's telling me.

"Crepes!" she says, scooting to the middle seat of the cab. Her leg brushes against mine, and that familiar lightning storm goes off all over my body. It was the same one that rolled in when I kissed her. I'm wondering if it will ever stop. I lean into the touch, not sure I want it to.

"Crepes?" I ask. "That's what you want?"

"It's very French." Georgia is leaning further into me and batting her eyelashes like she has to convince me. With her arm and shoulder pressed into my side, I can hardly think beyond the point of contact. There's no need to convince, I'd go anywhere as long as she kept touching me—talking to me.

"Thirteenth-century France, to be exact." I raise a brow at her, and she scoffs, leaning away and pressing her back into the seat.

"Of course, you know that." She's scrolling through her phone, looking for another place to eat as I put my arm behind her, taking the phone out of her hand and clicking on the address to the creperie she found.

"Why are you trying to find something else? I thought you said crepes?" I wink at her, and gods above, I hope it doesn't look stupid.

She'd probably tell me if it did.

The cab pulls away, and I am painfully aware of her presence in the car.

Without thinking, I take my arm off the seatback and put my hand on her thigh, close to her knee. Squeezing gently, I slide my eyes to hers and notice her expression. It's the same one she had before I kissed her. Lips parted, breath shallow, cheeks stained pink. I can't get enough of it.

She's messing with my mind, and true to our history, I can't wait to throw back everything she's thrown at me.

I lean in slightly, feeling my pulse quicken as my lips rest just an inch from hers. She sucks in a breath, and I let the smile split across my face. "We shouldn't kiss on the first date, Georgia," I whisper. "It would be in bad taste."

She scowls at me as I lean away, unable to wipe off my stupid grin. I squeeze her thigh gently again as we pull up to the restaurant and don't move my hand—not for anything.

Windows line the small café where Georgia and I sit. The black table is just small enough for my knees to brush hers beneath the surface, and I suddenly realize I haven't stopped touching her since we got in the car.

I can't stop thinking about touching her.

Fuck.

I don't know how I'm going to make it another night on the opposite side of that stupid mound of pillows. In fact, I have no idea what this entire day means, but whatever it is, I want it.

All of it.

Georgia orders crepes layered with Nutella and banana slices. The picture shows them covered in powdered sugar. I go for something savory since it's lunchtime, thankful that our waitress speaks English. I didn't want a repeat of pointing like an idiot in the way I had to at the café down the street from our hotel.

When our food arrives at the table, Georgia is staring at my plate. Her brows furrowed as I try not to laugh at her expression.

"Wait," she says. "Why does yours not look like a dessert?" Her eyes are flicking between me and my plate.

I chuckle, picking my fork up off the table. "Crepes aren't just for dessert." I roll my eyes when she gives me an infuriated look—like I'm flaunting some kind of knowledge I gained at culinary school.

It's not true. Most people know they aren't just dessert. I didn't need the schooling to know, but I don't dare say that to Georgia.

She may bite my head off.

And at this point, I'd thank her for it.

Shit. Get it together.

"These were off the lunch menu," I answer.

She picks up her fork, analyzing my food. "Shut up," she says. "Can I try some?" Her hazel eyes flick to mine, and there's literally no way I could say no.

I'm down bad.

When did that happen?

"Sure."

She doesn't waste time leaning forward and reaching around the small flowers at the center of the table to steal a bite of my food.

She groans as soon as the food reaches her mouth, and I have to fight every thought or image that instantly invades my mind. It doesn't help that I can still feel her leg brushing up against mine. "These are so good."

I smile and reach across the table, stealing a piece of her food and shoving it in my mouth. I don't regret agreeing to come here, and I'm honestly glad she picked this place— though I would have gone anywhere.

"It's only fair," I say, a satisfied smile on my face.

Georgia leans over the table, and I fight the urge to look down. I don't want to be an asshole—not now. "It's not fair when you could probably make these yourself."

I laugh because she doesn't realize just how easy these are. "I can make crepes," I say, sure she can read my expression and knows how desperately I want to make fun of her.

Sitting back, Georgia cuts into her food with the side of her fork as her tongue rolls along her cheek. "Well, aren't you just perfect?"

"I don't know about that." I take a bite of my food and shift forward to increase the contact between us beneath the table. I wonder if she even notices, and I hope she does because my skin is burning like fire. "You might be, though." My tone is matter of fact.

The flush on her cheeks lets me know I hit the mark. It was a dumb comment—overly cheesy and ridiculous, but I don't care. I told her I was taking her on a date, and I'm about to do just that.

"Coming on a little strong for a first date, don't you think?" Her eyes are lighted, and she fails to fight the corner of her lip that rises.

"I consider our first date the time I bought you a beer in exchange for feet pictures."

Georgia shushes me, her face horrified as she holds up a finger to my lips. "Shut up, or people are going to hear you and think you're serious." She sits back down.

"Well," I say, trying not to laugh. "I didn't say it in French."

She deadpans. "Our waitress spoke English."

The laugh finally escapes. "You might be right. So, Georgia." There's a joking tone to my voice. "Tell me about yourself."

She rolls her eyes and takes a sip of her water, the glass pressing against the very mouth I now know the taste of. "What do you want to know?"

I lick my lips, my brows creasing as a serious expression takes over my face. I'm practically interviewing her. "Preferably your hopes and dreams." I let my eyes flick down—just once, and all those filthy images are back. "Maybe a fun fact or two. Possibly an in-depth description of how you see our game of *Twister* going when you come over to my house."

Her cheeks are bright pink, and I can honestly say I've never seen Georgia nervous before. She's suddenly fidgeting with her utensils, keeping her hands busy. The fact that I'm the reason is definitely going to my head.

My ego is growing by the second.

She doesn't talk for a moment—chewing slowly. "I expect it to go like a game of *Twister*," she finally says, and I wonder if she's having the same thoughts I'm having. Probably not. They aren't very respectable, and she seems to have calmed down. "You'll fall on your ass, and I'll win."

Georgia raises her eyebrows in challenge, cutting off another piece of her crepe with her fork.

I grab my water and take a drink. "Do you fall down too?" I ask. "Because I would probably take you down with me." I lean forward to punctuate my next statement. "Out of spite."

Georgia's tone is mocking, rising and falling like a mountain range as she makes fun of my earlier comment. "That's very on brand for you."

"There's no way either of us would win," I admit. We've spent so much time battling things out by volleying insults back and forth that there's no way we would cave in to anything competitive. "I'm pretty sure we would sabotage the whole thing to win."

"Ah, ah." Georgia wags her fork at me. "Even if we both end up on the ground, I'd still win." She's clearly amused. "I'd be on top, of course."

My eyebrows could not shoot up higher. The room is suddenly too warm as I picture all the ways that would actually happen—her on top. I'd give anything to be beneath Georgia Clark right now.

Jesus Christ.

I can tell she realizes what she said because her mouth snaps shut. She doesn't need to stop, though.

I really don't want her to stop.

I drop my voice lower, rolling my tongue on the inside of my cheek. "Would you, now?" I ask, just to see if she is going to backtrack.

She shoves more food in her face and talks around a full mouth. It's enough to make me let out a breathy laugh and break some of the tension. "These crepes are delicious."

I run a hand through my hair, trying to dispel the energy in any way I can. "I can make you something better."

There's heat in her eyes when she looks at me, and I wonder if she might be thinking about being on top again.

Fuck. Fuck. Fuck.

I'm thinking about it again. "Food," I correct. "I can make you food."

"I only eat toddler food," she says. "Remember?"

Very on brand. "Then I will create a toddler masterpiece," I say. "You will be the star of the entire daycare with the lunch I pack for you."

Georgia laughs, and I decide I want to hear the sound again. Possibly for the rest of my life.

That might be too soon.

"You're going to be one of those crazy bento box moms that overdoes lunchtime for their kid, right?"

"Of course."

"Then I expect a nice note in my lunchbox, Mom."

I let my eyes trail over her again and shift in my chair—readjusting. "Whatever I write for you will not be nice." She's staring at me, and I'm not sure if the restaurant is on fire or not. It might be. I wouldn't know. It was warm earlier. Now it's boiling. "So," I say. "Hopes and dreams?"

Georgia shakes her head and clears her throat. "Right. Well, I'm becoming a teacher, aren't I?"

"And based on our breakfast, you really *do* want to be doing that."

During our first breakfast together, Georgia talked about all her students and their passions. She knows them all and clearly cares. I admire her for it.

I can see it in her eyes when she looks at me, the love for what she does. Her face is serious, and I notice the small freckle on her jawline when she talks. "More than you know." She looks down again, returning to her food, but she doesn't stop talking, and I find I want to listen. "I love my students," she confesses. "All of them. Even the shitty ones. I like watching them learn, of course, but more than that, I love getting to know them as people. I love seeing what they can do with their lives and watching them chase after their goals."

"Inspiring."

"Are you making fun of me?" Her brows crease, and I reach across the table, tracing my fingers over hers until she flips her hand over. I keep tracing patterns on her palm. I don't know what I'm drawing, but all I want is the contact—to be touching her—being here.

"I'm not making fun of you, Georgia. It is inspiring. It shows how much you care about people." My eyes finally meet hers. "Without expecting anything in return." I smile. She's always been there for Emerson, and I'm not surprised to hear that she's like that with everyone. Anna certainly wasn't like that—caring, that is. "We know how high schoolers can be. I was certainly an asshole."

"You still are."

"And you're still capable of liking me." It sounds more like a question—like vulnerability. I try not to wince. "At least, I hope."

God damn it.

I'm practically in high school all over again with how nervous she's making me. I'm afraid of saying the wrong thing—of ruining how things are now and returning to a time when she hated me.

"Yeah," she answers. "I am."

There's a comfortable silence that stretches between us when the waitress comes over. I'm pretty sure I say the word *what,* three times before I figure out that she's asking us if we want the check. I, of course, take it before Georgia can grab it.

"As for those hopes and dreams," she starts, continuing the conversation. "I'd like to not burn out in my first five years. But the way education is going, that's very likely."

"You won't." There's no way. She's too stubborn. "You're anything if not determined, Georgia." She's looking at me now, and whatever I see in her eyes has my chest tightening. "I'm certain that as long as you want to teach, you'll find a way to do it." I mean every word.

Georgia sits back, swirling the water in her glass and thinking. "Okay, Sawyer Owens. Hopes and dreams."

"Oh, you know." I shift in my chair, pulling at the hood of my sweatshirt to readjust it. "I plan to meet a rich older woman online, have her send me a weekly allowance, and quit my job to live my best life as a stay-at-home trophy husband."

"Ha. Ha." She doesn't look amused, and it brings another smile to my face.

"No." My brows furrow. I haven't talked much about what my plan is because I'm not sure I'd be able to do it. I've always been confident, but this is one area where I have a lot of doubt. Leo doesn't take any suggestions about menu items. He's great, otherwise, and a part of me wonders if it's because of *me.* "I'd like to be the head chef," I say. "I'd love to have more control over the menu at Catch 45." It's not the whole truth, and somehow, she sees it.

When I look up, Georgia tilts her head, raising a

brow. "That's all?" she asks.

I shove the feelings of self-doubt away. "Maybe open my own restaurant." I can't look at her—not as I say the words aloud.

"Will you make crepes?" she asks. "When you open your restaurant."

When.

There's no doubt there—only the assurance that I could run my own business. Somehow, that assurance coming from Georgia—the girl who has relentlessly insulted me since the day we met—means a lot.

Too much.

I don't want to figure out what that means.

She leans forward, folding her arms over the surface of the table. "They really are delicious."

I chuckle, scooting forward in my chair until our knees brush again. "Only if you promise to show up and eat them," I respond.

"I'll show up at your restaurant," she answers, smiling. It almost hurts. "And then we can go back to your house and play *Twister.*"

I raise my brows at the insinuation, and for whatever reason—

She doesn't try to take it back.

TWENTY

Georgia

When I get back to the hotel room with Sawyer closing the door behind me, I can only focus on the made-up bed resting in the center of the room. It's practically screaming at me.

I don't know what we are going to do.

In an effort to eradicate every dirty thought entering my mind, I sit on the end of the bed and try to figure out how to watch a movie.

"We're watching *Pride and Prejudice,*" I say. "After all that time at the castle, you need to appreciate Darcy's estate."

Sawyer is laughing as he throws himself on the bed, scooting back to prop up against the headboard.

God, he's beautiful.

And kind.

And funny.

Holy shit.

I turn away, fumbling with the remote until I finally find what I'm looking for.

"We can buy it!" I announce—almost too excited.

Sawyer is leaning back with an arm behind his head. His sweatshirt is riding up, revealing that sliver of skin above the waistband of his pants.

I think I might be panting.

It's embarrassing.

Without thinking too much, I move up to join him, adjusting the pillows behind me. When I look up at him, he's staring, a question in his gaze.

"Should we resurrect the great wall?" he asks. "I don't usually hop into bed with women on the first date." He winks, and my face warms. "I'm a gentleman, you know."

I try to laugh it off—to hide what all his comments are doing to me. All through lunch, he kept saying things that had my stomach flipping uncontrollably. "Shut up," I say, feigning irritation. "You said our first date was the time I sent you feet pics, anyway."

Sawyer wraps an arm around my shoulders and gently pulls me against him. I let him do it, relishing in the warmth of his body and the closeness as the movie plays on the television in the background.

Before Lizzy gets done walking while reading her book, I shoot up and pause the movie.

"Wait," I say, turning back to him. "Put your pj's on."

I hop off the bed, grabbing my night clothes from my bag. I'm smiling as I walk off to the bathroom to change, throwing my hair up in a bun, brushing my teeth, and pulling the oversized science t-shirt over my head.

I peel the contact lenses from my eyes because if I sleep in them, I may explode, catch fire—be framed for tax fraud. I don't really know—but my eye doctor makes it seem very, *very* bad.

Sliding on my leggings, I amble to the door before walking out into the hotel room. Sawyer is back on the bed in gray sweatpants and a black t-shirt. Looking like a god.

I could be drooling.

Why did I hate him again?

I grab our macarons out of the fridge and tuck in next to him, pressing the play button for the second time.

"You're going to like this," I say, looking up at him. I don't think I've been happier. This is one of my favorite movies, and that he is willingly watching it—

Sawyer rolls his eyes, but he can't hide the smile on his face. "I highly doubt *that*," he says.

~

"I don't understand why Lizzy is crying like that." Sawyer's brow creases. His arm rests around my shoulders, thumb brushing the skin beneath the sleeve of my t-shirt. I can hear his heartbeat from where my head rests on his chest.

"Because her sister ran away with Wickham," I answer as if it's the most obvious thing in the world.

Because it is.

"What's the problem with that?" he asks, and I sit up, twisting to get a better look at him.

Our macarons are gone, trash discarded on the

nightstand, and the room is dark as the sun sets behind the Paris skyline outside.

"It's improper! She will shame the entire family, for one. None of the girls will be able to marry respectable men! They will be outcasts in society."

Sawyer huffs a laugh. "Seems excessive." He runs a hand through his hair, mussing it in a way that has me biting my lip. "The entire family gets shamed?" he asks.

"Yes. She went with Wickham out of wedlock. It doomed the entire family."

"So dramatic." Sawyer is rolling his eyes, but I can see that underneath it, he likes the movie. If he didn't, he wouldn't be sitting here still watching it with me. I know that for sure.

"Don't worry," I respond, tucking myself back into my spot. "Darcy is about to fix everything."

"What a hero." He doesn't sound convinced.

As the movie continues, I find sleep calling my name. I do the one thing that secures the route of my current train to exhaustion city. I take my glasses off and set them on the nightstand.

When I reposition myself, Sawyer is running his fingers through my hair even as it's tied up, and I can't help the way it relaxes me. That lemongrass scent surrounds me, and his heart beats steadily in his chest, keeping time with the rhythm of my own.

I let myself close my eyes.

"Georgia?" he says, interrupting the haze of sleep that was falling over me.

"Hm?" I'm barely there.

"Why does he keep calling her Mrs. Darcy? He says it like so many times."

My mind briefly recalls the scene playing in the background. I keep my eyes closed and smile against his chest as Sawyer continues running his fingers over my scalp. The man could kill a woman like this.

I'd be happy to go.

"Because," I say, sleep thick in my voice. "He's completely and perfectly and incandescently happy."

I tuck my hand beneath his shirt to warm it, feeling his stomach beneath my cold fingers. Sawyer is athletic—fit, but there's a softness there—one that reminds me of all the good food he could make me.

Food like crepes and macarons.

I want him to cook for me.

I want to cook *with* him.

"I still don't understand," he says, tightening his grip on me.

"Then you're an idiot." I'm smiling now, my eyes still closed. "He's saying it because he is really, very happy."

Sawyer chuckles, and I can feel his stomach move beneath my fingers. His breath fans out over my face.

"Okay," he says, settling back more on our bed. There's a pause before he continues. "Okay, Mrs. Darcy."

I fall asleep to the sound of his breathing and the feel of his body beneath mine.

TWENTY-ONE

Sawyer

When I wake up, Georgia is still sleeping on my chest, one leg tossed over mine, and her hand tucked under my shirt.

Something about having her hand there, sprawled across my stomach, wakes me up. I can't get myself to focus on anything aside from her warm fingers resting below my pecs.

My heart is beating faster, my mind flashing images like a movie—is this the hand flex she was so obsessed with? The slightest touch from her is making me absolutely crazy. This must be what she was talking about.

I get it now, and I simply do not want to move.

I cannot move.

My phone buzzing across the room says otherwise.

I drag myself off the bed, carefully detaching her

from me before striding to the desk to get my phone. Georgia groans, stretching out to sleep on her stomach as I read the text message.

Warren: We'll be at breakfast in thirty minutes if you guys want to come. We can stop by. Bachelor party is tonight, and Sadie is doing something this afternoon. I think she wanted to ask Georgia to come.

"Georgia?"

Her eyes crack open before she moves to sit up. "Yeah?" Her voice is coated in sleep—raspy and tired as she licks her lips, rubbing her eyes briefly before looking at me.

Her gaze could set me on fire.

I clear my throat. "Warren and Sadie want to get breakfast with us in thirty minutes." I toss my phone on the end of the mattress, peeling my shirt over my head.

Once it's off, I notice Georgia staring. Her lips are parted, her eyes heated with the same intensity she had when we kissed yesterday.

God, I want to kiss her again.

"Was that necessary?" she squeaks before pressing her lips together and turning to look at the floor.

If my ego were any bigger, it would be its own planet.

"We have to get breakfast in thirty. I'm just changing." I lean down, rifling through my suitcase for something to wear. We planned on sightseeing together this morning, and I want to be comfortable.

"In here?" Georgia gets up, sliding off the bed and walking around to her suitcase by the armchairs. She bends over, and I fight the urge to watch her gather her things.

She's wearing leggings and—

Stop. You're practically a pre-pubescent boy right now.

Georgia turns and plants herself right in front of me, her hazel eyes flicking to my chest before rising to meet my gaze. I watch the way her breath catches, wondering if she's feeling the same things as I am, and if she doesn't stop, I'm not sure how much longer I'll be able to survive.

"You can't keep looking at me like that," I say. I'm vaguely aware of my own breath.

She steps forward, warmth washing over me at her closeness. I can feel her everywhere.

Georgia sticks her chin out in defiance. "Why not?"

I can't handle it anymore. I raise my hand, hesitating before slowly running my thumb along her jawline. Her skin is burning through me, and I can't help but think about how useless Smokey the Bear's job is about to be.

I want all the fire I can get.

"Because." I slide my hand back, moving my fingers to tangle in her hair as I lean down, my lips just inches from her ear. She leans in just slightly, and I know there is no way she can't feel this, too.

I like her.

A lot.

More and more with every new second I spend in her presence, and it makes me feel fucking stupid for ever hating her.

I drop my voice to a whisper, hoping to drive her just as wild as she is driving me. "This isn't our first date," I say. "There's only a matter of time before I do something about the way you're looking at me."

Georgia sucks in a breath as I turn to walk away. I pick up my clothes quickly, a satisfied smirk on my face as I enter the bathroom.

As soon as I close the door, I walk to the sink and let the water run. I want to know what she's thinking—what she wants, exactly. Maybe I could ask for specific instructions.

Fucking hell.

I'm so turned on.

I brush my teeth and slide on a pair of tan pants, pulling the muted blue Henley over my head and rolling up the sleeves. The weather has been mild, so I don't bother with a jacket after emerging from the restroom.

Georgia is already dressed and sitting on the armchair by the balcony, her hair draped over one shoulder. She stands up, moving around me with her toothbrush in hand. Before she walks through the door, I hear her say, "Maybe I'll make a move first."

And that, my friends, was the moment my heart stopped beating.

When she emerges, I'm already standing at the end of the bed. She smiles, adjusting her t-shirt before grabbing the keycard, tucking it in her jeans pocket, and turning to me. "We better head down for breakfast."

My heart is beating wildly in my chest, her words playing on repeat.

Maybe I'll make the first move.

Not likely. While things have changed between us in the past few days, I will never walk away from a challenge—not one Georgia has planted in my mind.

If I'm going to be stupid, I better be brave.

Before her hand grips the doorknob, I reach out, grabbing her waist and spinning her until her back hits the metal of the door.

She lets out a small whimper, our lips now inches apart. I drop my voice low, my eyes hooded as every nerve in my body screams for me to continue. "Don't challenge me, Georgia."

Her fingers dig into my hips, dragging me closer.

Shit.

"It seems to be working in my favor." Her voice is breathless, and whatever tension existed between us snaps.

My lips are on hers in an instant. Lightning shooting through my veins like a familiar storm—the same one that rolled in the moment she kissed me during that cooking class.

I trace my tongue along her bottom lip, relishing in the sound she makes as her fingers pull me even closer. It's like I've mapped out this specific reaction, the way we move together, and I cannot get enough. I'm pressed against her, hard, slowly losing my mind.

It will never be enough.

I kiss her harder, tangling my hand in her hair so I can grip the back of her neck.

When her hands slip beneath my shirt, my brain short circuits. There isn't a thought left when her palms slide over my chest. And certainly not when she leans into me, pressing her body closer—as if that were even possible.

I break the kiss, moving to trail my lips over her jaw—her neck—continuing to chart every inch of her skin, taking note of her reactions.

When I kiss beneath her ear, she moans and—

Fuck. *Fuck.*

I don't want to stop.

"We have to go to breakfast," she whispers. She's tilting her head to give me better access, and I hum my approval.

"Sure," I say, my mouth still ghosting over her soft flesh—an explorer.

"Didn't Warren text you?"

Her hands are in my hair, tugging gently as I push my knee between her legs and pull her away from the door. All I can think about is friction, and suddenly I'm dragging her forward. This new territory is my favorite of all my discoveries.

Georgia sucks in a sharp breath. "Shit," she whispers.

The knock on the door startles us both, my heart rising to my throat as we break apart quickly.

Georgia's lips are swollen, her cheeks pink, and her curly hair falling wildly around her shoulders. Trailing a finger over her bottom lip, she turns. "It's like each kiss gets even better," she whispers. "Maybe you're the poison."

I laugh, leaning over her to look through the hole and into the hallway where Warren and Sadie are waiting.

"They're here," I state, trying to straighten—I don't even know what. I'm sure we both look disheveled, like I've crossed the Sahara in search of my next great find.

"Good thing, too." Georgia plasters a smile on her face. "They saved me from an imminent death."

When Georgia turns, I quickly adjust myself. I am so

fucking hard, it's almost embarrassing. As the door opens, Georgia greets Sadie, tucking a strand of hair behind her ear.

I'm running my hands through my own brown strands, trying to get the feel of Georgia's body out of my mind—off of my skin.

"Did we interrupt?" Warren says as Sadie and Georgia stride down the hall in front of us. I shouldn't be embarrassed. Obviously, he believes Georgia and I have been dating for *seven fucking months.*

It would be normal—whatever occurred. But we haven't been dating—we aren't dating. I have no clue what we are doing.

I chuckle, but the sound is strained. "No, of course not."

"Right." He intones the word, like he doesn't believe any of the bullshit I just spewed.

I don't regret it at all. In fact, I think I'd sell my soul just to have my mouth on Georgia again.

"We're planning on going to an arcade," Warren says as we reach the elevators. "Sadie is taking a car to the Loire Valley around one. It's a three-hour drive."

"I'd like you to come!" Sadie is looking at Georgia and waiting for a response. Her dark eyes lighted with hope. "We're doing a wine tasting down there. There will be a small party, then we will head back to Paris for the night."

When we get into the elevator, Georgia grabs my hand, her fingers weaving through mine naturally. "Sounds great," she says, one eyebrow cocking. "I love wine."

I squeeze her hand once before we exit the elevator and make our way to breakfast.

~

Emerson: I didn't hear from either of you yesterday. Did one of you finally snap? Did Georgia strangle you?

I look down at my phone as I take another sip of coffee. It isn't as good as the fancy café down the street, but it's decent.

Sadie and Warren already took off to prepare for whatever is going on later today, and Georgia sits across from me, eating a piece of bread filled with chocolate—the only breakfast item this hotel seems to offer.

"Emerson texted me."

Georgia's eyes snap up. "About?"

"She's asking if we've strangled each other. What do I say?" I sit back in my chair, tapping my finger on the wooden surface of the table. I'm not sure what I should say.

Well, Nemo. I had a raging hard-on this morning while I kissed your best friend against the door of our hotel room. My hands may be around her neck, but not in the way you're thinking.

That seems like too much.

The room where guests eat breakfast has filled up considerably—couples and families chatting at the wooden tables littering the vast space.

"Do I tell her we made out against the door?"

"No." Georgia looks panicked. "We should ease her into—" She gestures like she's trying to find the right word, but nothing seems to stick. "I don't care what you say, but she doesn't need to know about—" Georgia looks away, clearing her throat. "She doesn't need to know specifics."

A smirk pulls at my lips. "Whatever you say, princess." I pull out my phone, typing out a response.

Me: Quite the opposite.

Cryptic.
Not forthcoming with information.
Not a lie.
It's the perfect way to ease her into it.
Emerson's response is almost immediate, and I open the text message.

Emerson: Wtf is that supposed to mean?

Me: It's going well, Nemo. I'll call you tonight.

"What did you tell her?" Georgia is picking up her own cup of coffee, blowing on the steaming surface. I can feel it all over again, and I have to adjust in my seat.

"I just told her it was going well and I'd call her." I raise an eyebrow. "Don't worry," I say before dropping my voice lower. Not that it matters. Most of the guests are speaking other languages. "I didn't tell her about the insanely hot kiss."

Georgia huffs out a breath before taking a sip of her coffee. "Right," she says. "The kiss. That's all." She doesn't seem convinced.

I roll my tongue along my cheek, leaning back in the chair. "That's all," I repeat. "So far."

The look of shock on her face is enough to stoke the flames. I don't think I will ever stop making lewd comments. Not when she looks so beautiful with her cheeks pink, her eyes blazing from brown to green.

"I need to get a gift for Sadie," she says, breaking the tension. "Do you want to come with me?"

I lean forward, grabbing a piece of bread and taking a bite. I swallow before speaking again. "We could see the Eiffel Tower. You didn't get to when I went. I think you should see it." I cock an eyebrow. "From the top."

Georgia almost chokes on her coffee, wiping her mouth with a napkin. "I really want to see it at night." Her tone is level despite her earlier reaction, and something about it unsettles me. She's going to toss something back. I know it. "You know—when it's all lit up."

I chuckle at her response. "We can do that too."

"So, Eiffel Tower and lingerie shopping."

Yep.

It's my turn to choke. "Lingerie?" My voice cracks. There's no way I'm going lingerie shopping.

Not with Georgia Clark.

Not with the memory of her soft lips on mine, her fingers in my hair.

"For Sadie," she says, as if it's the most obvious thing in the world. "For her bachelorette party."

I wince. "Absolutely not. I will not help you pick out *lingerie* for my best friend's wife." I'm nearly whispering the words to keep guests from hearing.

"You're a guy," Georgia says, her tone even. "You'll know what to pick better than I will."

"I'm sure you can figure it out. I'll wait outside."

Georgia dips a spoon into her coffee, adding a packet of sugar and stirring. The look she gives me is enough to bring me to my knees.

It's what she says afterward that would have me kissing the ground she walked on, too.

"Don't you want to see me try stuff on?"

I don't think my brain is working.

I'm just staring.

I'm—

Shit.

I adjust in my seat, trying to hide what that very enticing image just did to me.

"Do they let you leave the dressing room in that stuff? I don't think they'd let you walk out of the dressing room."

"That's fine," she says, still looking at her coffee. "I'd be happy to send pictures."

If my brain wasn't working before, I now fully identify as a vegetable.

TWENTY-TWO

Georgia

Sawyer was right about the Eiffel Tower.

Despite the crowd, it was still amazing. From the top, we could see the entire city below. Sawyer kept pointing out the different landmarks, smiling when he got to the arc.

"And that's where you nearly passed out because you didn't have your nap and a meal," he said.

I rolled my eyes at that one, but there was no loathing—not anymore. It kind of scared me.

We also took numerous pictures together. If he was worried about people seeing them before, he didn't seem to care now.

The most difficult part of our morning outing was finding a lingerie shop in Paris, but somehow, we managed.

"We don't have a lot of time," I say, moving to the wall displaying bras in every size imaginable. I don't know what Sadie's size is. We aren't exactly best friends, and I don't spend our moments together staring at her boobs.

"Hey," I say, my brows furrowing as I turn to Sawyer. "Do you know—" I cut myself off. I laugh a little at his horrified expression. I wonder if he knows what I was about to ask. "Never mind."

Too bad bras can't be a one-size-fits-all deal.

I don't even think they're a many-sizes-fit-all.

A man definitely invented them.

I should look that up later.

I walk past different mannequins and display tables, glancing at the price tag on a pair of underwear.

Holy shit.

Good thing Sawyer has been paying for stuff, or I wouldn't be able to afford this gift.

Speaking of—I wonder if he thinks I'm a gold digger. I'm not. I—

"I'm paying for this gift. Just so you know."

"Look, Georgia." Sawyer moves in front of me, blocking me from getting to the back of the store. His body is warm, and I'm instantly brought back to how it felt to have him pressing against me. My stomach flutters. "I don't mind paying for stuff. I saved for this trip, but I wasn't going to offer to pay for lingerie for my best friend's wife."

I bite my lip, trying to hold back the smile. "You'd be doing him a real—" I pause, trying to emphasize the next word so he catches my meaning. "Solid," I say.

"Ha." He's tilting his head to the side and looking down at me. "That's a good one."

I lean in just a hair, sticking my chin out. "That was a great joke."

I walk around him, determined to find a nightgown or a robe I can buy—something I know will fit Sadie.

I spot gold silk out of the corner of my eye and make a b-line for the nightgowns on the far wall. "This one," I say, grabbing it off the rack.

I check the price tag and nearly vomit. I can still do it, though. It'll be fine as long as I don't throw up on the garment I'm holding.

"Are you sure?" Sawyer asks, stepping closer.

"Yeah. It's a little pricy, but I think it'll work."

Sawyer licks his lips, leaning over until I'm staring up into his brown eyes, my body buzzing. "You don't want to try that on, do you?"

He inches closer, his lips inches from mine. My gaze flicks down before I meet his, and every ounce of my being crying out to touch him.

Sawyer's hand is warm when it lands on my waist, pulling me forward as I hold the nightgown away from us. "Georgia." His voice is almost pained—raspy and making me want to strip down in the middle of the store.

I know what his body feels like, at least a little. That kind of knowledge is not power in this situation.

It's rendering me completely powerless.

A woman speaking French has us breaking apart. It takes me a second to register that she works here when I turn to see her red painted lips moving, hair tied back in a neat bun. I can't for the life of me figure out what she's saying.

"I'm sorry?" I say before clearing my throat, trying to gather my thoughts.

"Puis-je vous aider?"

My brows furrow. I am literally rubbing every last brain cell together, trying to remember my high school French classes.

I might very well be an idiot.

One word sticks out to me. *Aider.*

Help. She's asking if we need help.

I try to think of a word—any word to offer her. I'm not sure if I get the right one, but I try it out anyway, hoping that Madam Boyd won't shame me for the rest of my natural life should she catch wind of what occurred on this fine day in Paris. She was a very strict teacher.

"Acheter?" It sounds like a question. "I think." I give her my best *I'm sorry I'm an American* smile. "Can I buy this?"

The woman laughs, her accent thick when she switches to English. "Yes, ma'am," she says. "I appreciate your French." She gestures for us to follow. "Allons-y."

Giving a satisfied smile, I look at Sawyer as if I've single-handedly found the cure for cancer. I can't wait to receive all of my prizes and medals as we follow her to the register.

"I bet you're feeling proud of yourself," he whispers before we get to the counter. "All that time watching the French soap opera prepared you for this exact moment."

"I'd like to think I learned something in high school," I retort. "We don't have a lot of time before Sadie's bachelorette party. Do you think they can wrap this up?"

"I don't know," Sawyer says, humor laced in his tone. "Use your French skills and see if you can ask."

"You know what?" I say, turning to him. I tilt my head to the side. "I think I will."

It's a good thing Sawyer doesn't speak French, because I know as soon as I open my mouth, I totally butcher it.

It isn't all bad, though. We still end up with one fantastic gift, and some fantastic dirty thoughts.

TWENTY-THREE

Sawyer

Georgia left as soon as we returned to the hotel after Sadie accosted her in the lobby. Surprisingly enough, Georgia didn't seem to mind.

I suppose it made sense since she's friends with my sister. Emerson is the queen of accosting people when she's overly excited.

I'm pretty sure that's how Georgia ended up on this trip to begin with.

I laugh, running my hand down my face as I wait in the lobby for Warren and his two friends. I don't know the other guys. He must have met them in Nevada, and I'd be lying to say I wasn't a little nervous.

Warren and I haven't had a chance to really catch up, and I'm hoping I don't feel off at whatever this bachelor party is.

He mentioned an arcade, and I figured I could get

lost in games and it wouldn't matter.

"Hey, man. You ready?" Warren smacks my back once before appearing with two others. "This is Nash and Ian. They're coworkers."

After shaking hands with the tall red-head and the shorter blonde guy, I smile at Warren. "I'm sure all three of us will thoroughly enjoy kicking your ass at this arcade. You're the groom, which means you're the target."

"He's got a point," Nash says, laughing. "Ian and I already did the marriage thing. This is your show, buddy."

"Well, Sawyer's got a girl," Warren says. "Speaking of, what's your plan with that?"

My mind goes blank.

Is he asking—

"You think about a ring, yet?"

No.

According to Warren, Georgia and I have been dating for seven months. I guess it wouldn't be unthinkable to plan on proposing at this point.

The only problem is Georgia and I aren't really dating at all—which makes it unthinkable.

I can't let him know that now, though, so I opt for lying—my favorite thing. "I've thought about it."

I have not thought about anything. I wasn't even thinking about it with Anna.

"Oh, shit," Ian says, folding his arms across his chest. The guy may be shorter, but he's built. "Paris would be a good place to make it happen."

I am scrambling here. Alarm bells are ringing. It's like *Mission Impossible*, and I was completely unsuccessful. I have triggered every trip wire.

Every. Single. One.

I shake off the feelings with a casual laugh. "Not here," I say, trying to find some truth to cling to. "It's a little too soon."

"I proposed to my wife after like four months," Nash says. "When you know, you know, man."

Right.

"Well, this is Warren's wedding," I say, trying to dig out of whatever hole I landed in. I don't even remember digging it.

No, I do. I dug it the second I showed up at Georgia's school with this bright idea, and now it's ten kinds of complicated.

"So, rehearsal dinner tomorrow, and then the big day," I say as we all start walking to the exit.

"Holy shit," Warren says, a wide smile stretching across his face.

"Holy shit is right," Nash adds, chuckling. "Just wait. Before you know it, you'll be twenty pounds heavier and waking up four times a night."

"You have kids, I take it?" I ask.

"Yeah." He blows out a breath. "Two. This is quite the vacation for me and Kristin. She's a mess, though. It's her first time away from the gremlins." He rubs the back of his neck. "I'd be lying to say I wasn't a mess, too. They're with her parents."

"Well, I'm glad you're here," Warren confesses as we walk out to the sidewalk.

A black SUV waits at the curb as the driver walks

around to open the door. We all pile in and get settled before the car starts moving.

I pull out my phone when we get in the cab, finding a text from Georgia.

It's six in the evening. They should be heading back soon.

> **Georgia:** You're not supposed to drink the wine. Did you know that? I didn't know.

I chuckle, hiding my smile as I run my hand down my face.

Oh shit.

Another text comes through, then another.

> **Georgia:** I drank a lot of it.
> **Georgia:** She loved the nightgown. You have good taste. I think I should get one for myself.

I clear my throat, ignoring whatever conversation is happening around me and trying to think of a way to reply.

Georgia beats me to it.

> **Georgia:** I could wear it in our room. I only packed two sets of pjs.

> **Me:** You cannot wear that.

> **Georgia:** Don't tell me what to do, Sawyer. I'll sleep how I want. Maybe I won't wear anything. You can't boss me around.

Fuck.

It's going to be a long night.

~

Warren has made some good friends since moving, and I couldn't be happier for him—or more thankful because I don't feel out of place with Nash and Ian.

We spent the entire night catching up, drinking beers, and killing a ridiculous number of zombies.

I can honestly say it's the most fun I've had in a while. I've been busting my ass at the restaurant—mostly to prepare for this trip but also in the hopes of gaining Leo's approval.

As soon as I get back to the hotel room, though, I see Georgia sprawled out on the bed, still wearing the dress she picked out earlier.

She's already passed out, and I'm trying my best not to laugh while thinking of the texts she sent earlier.

I quietly grab my sweats, and pull them on, not bothering with a shirt before I sit on the edge of the bed.

"Georgia," I say. "You're going to have to make some room."

She groans, rolling over. Her eyes are still closed when she speaks. "Alcohol makes me hot. Like the temperature."

I chuckle. "I'm sure."

"Can you help me take my dress off? It's really hot in here." She stretches her arms over her head, and I swallow.

"I think you'd like to undress me, anyway."

Fuck. Shit. Holy fucking shit.

"I—"

"That's probably not a good idea," she says. "I'll just sleep in this."

"Yeah," I swallow again—hard. "Probably not a good idea."

Not while she's drunk. Definitely not while she's drunk. She is right about one thing, though. I would love to undress Georgia Clark. A week ago, I would have never thought—

Georgia rolls over until she's facing away from me.

"Do you want blankets?" I ask. "Since alcohol makes you hot, I wasn't sure." I can't help the smirk on my face.

"Yeah," she says as she lies on her stomach. She lifts one leg, her dress riding up, and I'm trying so hard not to look. I really don't want to be an asshole right now, so I just pull the blankets up over her before crawling in.

"I want you to press me against the door again," she says.

Why is she doing this to me?

"Yeah?" My voice is raspy, rough around the edges as I try not to think about what she's saying. There's no way I would do anything with her in this state, but I can't lie. I want to press her against the door, too—feel her body pressed against mine—watch her come undone.

"Yeah, and I want you to touch me. I wanted you to touch me that first day at dinner."

I practically groan. She has to stop talking.

"I need to sleep," she finally says. "But later. You can

touch me later, Sawyer. I'll show you how later."

God damn.

"Sure," I say, not fully believing the words leaving her mouth. She must have had a lot of wine. It doesn't stop the thoughts, though. "Goodnight, Georgia."

With all of the images playing on repeat in my mind—the ones that would have my mother signing me up for some kind of exorcism—there is no way I'm going to be falling asleep anytime soon.

Not tonight, at least.

TWENTY-FOUR

Georgia

The sun streaming in from the balcony window is a dickwad—a complete and utter dickwad

I groan, covering my head with a pillow to block out the light before registering where I am.

I abruptly prop myself up on my elbows, looking around the room and noticing that Sawyer is gone.

My brows furrow before I glance down at the dress I'm still wearing—the one from the bachelorette party.

I throw myself down, huffing out a breath as details slowly trickle in. We went to the wine tasting at a vineyard in the Loire Valley, and it was hopelessly fun, but I'm an actual idiot. Emerson would make fun of me relentlessly. She will never let me live this down if she finds out.

Sadie brought her friends Kristin, Zoe, and Ivy along with us. Kristin and Zoe were married to Warren's friends, and Ivy and Sadie had been friends since birth—possibly conception. I should have felt like an outcast, but I didn't.

That is, until I realized we were supposed to spit the wine out.

It was really quite good.

I grab my phone, noticing a missed call from Emerson. Since the room is empty, and I have nothing better to do, I call her back.

"What was Sawyer talking about?" she asks. No *hello, Georgia. How is your trip going?*

"Hey to you, too. Also, what are you talking about?" I slowly sit up before dragging myself out of bed and to the bathroom to brush my teeth. I think an animal died in my mouth overnight. My hair is a mess, and I probably need a shower.

"Sorry," she says. "I really miss you, but what did my brother mean by *quite the opposite* when I asked if you had killed each other?"

I drop my toothbrush on the counter, whispering a curse. "When did he say that?"

"Yesterday. Would have been around breakfast for you."

We are going to have to tell her. I made out with her brother. He had me pinned against the door to our hotel room with all of his—*everything*—pressed against me. Sawyer had his lips on mine, and the things he was saying—

The things *I* was saying—

You can touch me later, Sawyer. I'll show you how later.

Oh. My. God.

"I don't know what he was talking about." My cheeks are on fire as I cover the phone with my hand, mouthing a

203

creative string of curse words. I can't believe I told him that. I can't believe I—

"Georgia?"

"I'm sorry, E. What did you say? I'm trying to brush my teeth."

"I was just saying you haven't sent me pictures yet! I need to see the adventures you're going on so I can live vicariously through you." I hear shuffling sounds in the background before a beeping noise from what I assume to be our microwave. "I had a great show last night," she says. "I wish you were there because I don't know what I'm doing with my life. Being alone in the apartment has me thinking all sorts of thoughts."

I plunge the toothbrush in my mouth with toothpaste on it and start brushing, trying to talk anyway while I erase the dead animal stench. "What kinds of thoughts?"

"I don't know. I've spent almost four years getting the marketing degree, and I—"

I spit in the sink and turn Emerson on speakerphone. My heart clenches in my chest. She has loved performing since I've known her. Emerson is happiest with music surrounding her, and though I think she would be good at anything she wanted to do, I've seen the way her job at the bar has lit her up—brought her joy.

"You don't want a job in marketing," I say, my tone soft. "E—"

"What the fuck am I doing?" she squeaks. "I just wasted four years of my life." I hear the microwave door open and close as I lean over the sink, staring at the phone.

"You haven't wasted your life." I smile and hope she can hear it in my voice. "You got me out of the deal."

"You're right. I'm sorry I'm bringing this up. You just haven't been here to talk. It doesn't change that I want all your pictures. Every last one."

Maybe not the one of your brother kissing me. You might not be ready for that.

"It's all right." I hear the door to the hotel room open, nerves coursing through my body. I still can't believe what I said to Sawyer last night, and I don't know if I'm ready to face him yet.

"I have to go, E. Sawyer just walked in, but I will say this. Whatever you want to do, regardless of what the plan was, you should do it. If you want to sell pet rocks on the internet, you know I'd support you."

"I would make the rocks very cute. Googly eyes and tons of glitter." I can hear her smiling and it eases something in me. "Tell Sawyer I said hi, and let him know I need his photos, too. I seriously wish I were there."

I chuckle, wiping my hands on the towel hanging by the sink. "I will. Lots of love."

"Ew, you sap." She's laughing. "Love you too, Georgia."

When the phone disconnects, I walk out into the bedroom to see Sawyer sitting in one of the armchairs with two coffees. He stands up quickly, eyes flicking around the room like he's trying to find anything to save him.

I wince.

Oh, awkward.

"I got you a drink," he says.

"Sawyer." I clear my throat. "I don't drink alcohol very much."

He lets out a tense laugh. "Clearly. Do you—" He's looking at me now, brown eyes asking a question I don't want to answer. I just know I'm cringing. "Do you remember—"

"Yeah." I don't let him finish. "I do. That was very sloppy drunk of me."

He walks over, holding my drink out, and my fingertips brush his when I take it. A jolt runs through me at the touch.

"I didn't mind it." His smile has relief washing over me. "Clearly," he adds. "I'm the one who pressed you against that door, and I'd be happy to oblige any requests to do it again. Since you're sober, of course." His eyes narrow. "You are sober, correct?"

I take a drink of my coffee. "Of course. I just have a throbbing headache."

"Oof. Is this a bad time to tell you I bought tickets for a boat ride after Warren and Sadie's dinner?"

"A boat ride?"

"You wanted to see the Eiffel Tower all lit up. I figured it would be cool to see it from the river. Well, I didn't figure. The lady at the desk said it would be cool. Her English was great." He gives me a wide smile, and I think my chest cracks open.

The warmth running through me at his gesture is something different—something deeper.

What the fuck?

"We're going to see the tower?" My voice is weak,

and I don't know what to think or feel about Sawyer's thoughtfulness.

"Yeah, tonight." He moves over to the edge of the bed, kicking off his shoes. "For now, you should probably work on getting rid of that headache. Do you want to watch something?"

Whatever feeling is happening inside me has to do with far more than just finding Sawyer attractive—and honestly? That's the scariest part of all.

The wind has been knocked out of me at the realization. Like expecting the bottom step and finding nothing but air.

"Should we go for the soap opera?" I ask.

He pats the bed next to him, and I sit, leaning back against the headboard.

One of his arms stretches behind his head while the other points the remote at the television to browse movies to rent.

"I was thinking we could go for something else. There's another one of those Jane Austen movies on here."

"Which one?" I ask before taking another sip of coffee. I'm pretty sure I need an IV of this stuff to get rid of my headache.

"*Emma*, I think. I haven't seen that one." He enters the name into the search bar and the movie pops up.

"It's great. Mr. Knightly and Emma fight all the time." I pull the blankets over my legs, tucking myself back into the bed.

"Oh, so they end up fucking?"

My eyes whip to his, and I get the sense that he might

be asking something else. With every comment—every action, I am wrapping myself even tighter around his finger.

Can you help me take my dress off?

Sawyer is staring at me, his eyes slowly heating like the temperature of the room.

I want him so badly it is physically painful. I mean, I am feeling actual pain staring at him sprawled out on the bed, asking me about a fictional couple and if they have sex or not.

"There are no sex scenes," I say. "But yeah, I assume they do."

He clicks on the movie and confirms the rental. "Perfect," he says, the smile still lingering on his face. "This is the one, then."

Oh boy.

TWENTY-FIVE

Sawyer

"So, how are we handling the Emerson thing, exactly?" Georgia's fingers weave through mine as we walk the glistening city streets.

It rained earlier, and as night fell, the sky cleared to reveal the perfect weather for a calm boat ride along the river running through Paris.

I don't even remember what it's called, but that's just fine. I couldn't care less at this point.

"What do you mean?" I ask.

She stops, letting go of my hand and wincing when she looks at me. "I don't really know what's going on here." She waves a hand between us. "With this."

"Well, according to Warren and his friends, I should be proposing by now."

Whatever sound Georgia makes—it resembles a distressed animal. "What?"

I rub the back of my neck, my stomach dropping to the damp street beneath my tennis shoes. "Okay, bad timing for a joke."

I can see the loading dock behind her where we will get on the boat. People wait in line, couples holding hands and whispering into each other's ears. I think—

I might want that.

With Georgia.

I might even want more, and that thought almost scares me the most. Whatever Warren suggested, I can see that becoming a possibility. It's something I hadn't thought about with Anna.

"So?" she questions.

Stepping forward, I put my hands around her waist and drag her closer. "I like you, Georgia." It's the truth, and the longer I'm with her, the louder that truth becomes.

I like her a whole fucking lot.

"I actually recall you saying you hated me." She cocks an eyebrow, holding back a smirk.

"Nah," I say, gripping the side of her face and leaning down. Her lips are just inches from mine, and the scent of pears fills my lungs. "I couldn't hate you."

"So," she whispers. "What are we doing?" Georgia closes her eyes as if she's afraid of the answer.

It's not like I haven't thought about it—what things could be like when we get back home. I don't think I could go back to hating Georgia Clark if I tried, and something in the way my chest swells at the thought of our trip to Versailles, at every barb she throws at me, tells me that maybe I'm capable of more than liking her, too.

"What do you want to do?" I'm trying to keep my tone even, keep the nerves out of my voice. "Because I'd like to keep seeing you after—" I run my thumb along her jawline, and she leans into the touch, giving me hope. "After we get back," I finish.

"See me how?"

"Naked, for one." Her eyes snap open, and she's scowling. That swelling feeling in my chest grows larger. "I'd like to date you. For real."

I can see the tension leave her shoulders. "I'd like to date you too, Sawyer."

"Good." I lean in, brushing my lips against hers. I can feel the kiss everywhere, all at once. It's consuming me from the outside in, filling cracks I didn't know had formed. "I'd still like to see you naked," I whisper against her lips.

Her fingers tighten on my hips, just subtly, but enough for me to notice. "I'd like to see the damn tower."

I place one more kiss on her smiling lips before reeling back. "Well, then." The scariest thought occurs to me as I look down at the beautiful woman before me. I would give her anything—in this moment, I couldn't say no. "What are we waiting for?" I question. "Let's go see your damn tower."

~

The boat ride lasts about an hour, and when we pass the glittering landmark, Georgia's eyes are wide. She takes about a thousand pictures and forces me to do the same—insisting that I'm the backup in case all of hers are blurry.

When we get off the boat, we decide to walk until the tower is standing tall in the distance where we can see it.

"Can you take a picture for us?" Georgia says to a couple passing. They look confused, and she holds out her phone, muttering some words I assume are supposed to be French.

Her accent is terrible.

"Oh!" The woman says, grabbing Georgia's phone.

Her fingers lace through mine as she drags me to the perfect spot, wrapping one arm around my back at my waist for the photo.

We smile, and I assume they took the picture already, but I hold up a finger, asking for one more.

I tip her back in front of the Eiffel Tower, kissing her cheek once as her arms wrap around my neck. I bring my lips to her ear. "Did you ever buy that nightgown for yourself?"

When we are both standing straight, Georgia takes her phone back and refuses to meet my eyes.

"No," she whispers. Her cheeks are flushed, and I want to kiss the shade—kiss her everywhere.

My eyes trace her every curve as my entire body tightens. "If I tell you to wear it, will you vow to sleep naked again?"

Georgia bites her lip. "You don't have to ask me to sleep naked."

My brows raise.

"We should go," she says as her eyes finally meet mine—laced with the intensity of a thousand fires.

Hell.

"Yep," I say. "Let's go." I grab her hand before whisking her back to the hotel as fast as humanly possible.

TWENTY-SIX

Georgia

As soon as the door closes, my back is against the door, and Sawyer's lips are covering mine and driving me insane.

My entire body is buzzing as his hands tuck beneath my shirt, rough palms running over my torso and making me cry out for *more*. My breath is coming out in shallow pants, and my back is arching as his tongue runs along my lower lip.

He pulls back. "This okay?" he asks.

"Yes," I breathe as he pulls the shirt up over my head. I couldn't say no if I wanted to. It's like every moment, every lingering touch has led to this moment, and my mind is suddenly filled with all the reasons I like Sawyer Owens—all the reasons everything about this is so right.

"Jesus, Georgia." His pupils are blown out as he looks at me, and suddenly, his lips are on mine again. One hand gently moves to the side of my neck, his thumb tracing my throat in a way that has me shivering.

"What?" I whisper between kisses, begging to know what he's thinking. My hands are on him, peeling off his shirt, desperate for more contact. He moves us from the door to the wall, his weight leaning into me. I take a moment to admire whatever piece of art stands before me. "We haven't been to the Louvre, yet."

Sawyer's laugh vibrates as he trails kisses down my neck. "That's what you're thinking about?"

"I was actually thinking that you look like art." I run my fingers over his pecs, down his stomach, and to the waistband of his jeans.

"That is so cheesy." His mouth is moving lower— lower—until his lips press against the swell of my breast. I moan at the contact.

"Shut up," I say, arching even more.

I can feel his chuckle all over my skin, his mouth still moving lower until he's pulling the cup of my bra down with his fingers. "Still good?" he asks.

I lean my head back against the wall. "Still good," I respond. Is it even a question? "Keep going. I want you to touch me."

His tongue is dragging over my nipple, one hand running up my spine as he pulls me closer.

I'm going to lose my mind like this. Everything feels good—too good. I knew he would feel like this. Somehow, in the back of my mind, I knew it would be like this from the moment he whispered in my ear at that first dinner. And now, adding in everything else, it's all almost too much.

Almost.

"I think I recall you offering some instruction on that matter," he whispers.

"What?" I say, my mind a muddied mess—no thoughts aside from detecting harsh breaths, and the zips of pleasure racing over my skin.

"When you were drunk. You told me you'd show me how to touch you."

Sawyer's lips are on my jaw now as I move my hand to the pockets of his jeans, dragging him closer. I can feel every inch of him against me, hardened and ready.

I may die tonight, I think. *It's okay. I'll be happy.*

Sawyer draws back, and I whimper at the loss of contact.

"Bed," he says, nodding in the direction of the mattress.

I scramble over, trying to contain myself. I don't think I've ever been more wound up. This trip was my second sexual awakening, I'm sure of it. I started out with hatred in my heart, and now I'm practically begging Sawyer to do anything and everything to me.

With one word, he has me racing to obey.

Fuck.

My head hits the pillow, and I arch up to unclasp my bra, tossing it to the floor because who needs it?

Sawyer's eyes are hungry, and I can see how much he wants this in the way he licks his lips—the way his pupils are taking over the brown color in his blazing eyes. I want it, too.

"Pants," he demands.

I work to peel off my jeans, throwing them to the floor as if they've personally offended me.

"All right," Sawyer says, staring down at me with a wicked glint in his eye. "I'm ready for you to teach me, Miss Clark."

"Oh, that is *so* inappropriate," I respond, rolling my eyes. It doesn't do a damn thing to stop the *want* inside of me.

He leans over the bed, his knee sliding up between my thighs, his arms caging me in. "I want to make sure I do everything exactly right." He leans down to kiss the center of my stomach, lower—lower.

My fingers tighten around the sheets, my eyes fluttering closed as he keeps moving down until he kisses right above the waistband of my underwear.

"I don't want to mess it up," he whispers, and I feel his breath fan over my pebbled skin. "Please, show me how to touch you, Georgia."

He sits up, eyes blazing, as he hovers over me. His gaze flicks to my hand still gripping the sheets for dear life. My heart is thrashing in my chest. I've never done *this* before—what he's asking. Somehow, I can't seem to care, not when he's looking at me like I was the one who personally lit the Eiffel Tower tonight.

I move my hand over my stomach, skating over my flesh—lower—lower, still.

I think Sawyer has stopped breathing, and I'm half tempted to call his bluff, but something about the way he's making me feel—the nagging voice inside my head that says this is about to be the best sex of my life pushes me onward.

"You still want me to show you?" I ask.

He nods, his arms trembling on either side of me as

he tracks my movements—hungry.

When my fingers land exactly where I need them, pleasure hits me. I can't look away from his expression, the way his full lips are parted, his eyes hooded and dark.

It is good—everything about this is good.

I'm already moving faster, the pleasure building as a gasp exits my lips.

"Yeah?" Sawyer whispers, and I know I'm not going to last. I squeeze my eyes shut until his fingers wrap around my wrist, dragging my hand away and making me whimper.

"I think I got it," he says, his voice thick with desire.

He sits up, shedding the rest of his clothes before leaning on one elbow beside me. His hand is suddenly between my thighs, and I gasp at the contact.

"Shit," I mutter.

He's beautiful—hopelessly so. He is also a quick learner. I'm panting as he drags his fingers over my clit before plunging them inside.

Sawyer kisses my chest, his hands still working between my legs—motions slow and fluid. "Is this right?" he says, his tongue flicking over my breast. I almost shutter.

"It's—*fuck*—yeah. It's right."

Everything inside me is winding tighter as he slides his fingers over me, plunging inside, and then dragging them back out.

My legs are shaking, and I'm almost embarrassed at the noises exiting my mouth. My hand shoots up, trying to cover the sounds.

Sawyer moves, warm fingers gently wrapping around my hand to remove it. "Let it out," he whispers. "I need to know how I'm doing."

Fuck.

He's back on me in an instant, my release building quickly as I gasp for air. "Shit," I whisper, my brows pinching together. "I'm going to—"

"Hm?" he says, his mouth trailing over my neck, my jaw. "You're going to what, Georgia?" I can feel his smile against my throat.

I don't get a chance to answer. My entire body is shaking as he takes me over the edge, my eyes squeezing shut.

When I open them, Sawyer is looking at me, his brown gaze molten, lips parted, and I just can't handle him like this—I can't—

"I want you," I whisper, moving my hand until my palm is dragging over his length. "I want you now."

He hisses at the contact, his eyes fluttering closed for a brief second. "I—Georgia." He looks pained. "I didn't bring anything." He grunts, leaning into my touch. "I wasn't exactly expecting—"

Oh. *Oh.*

"It's okay," I say. "If you're clean, it's fine. I'm good. I'm on birth control, too."

He looks over me for a moment, registering what I said before the realization releases him. He's on me in an instant, his mouth on mine, and his body hard against me.

It's like I can feel him everywhere. Burrowing beneath my skin until I'm so full, I don't even know what life was without him.

"You're beautiful," he whispers, and that feeling in

my chest swells.

He pushes closer. "You're sure?" he asks. I can feel him *there*—waiting.

"I'm sure."

"I meant what I said, Georgia." One of his hands brushes my hair away from my forehead, and my heart aches at the way he's looking at me. "I really, *really* like you."

I push myself upward and place a quick kiss on the corner of his mouth. There's only one truth echoing inside my head, so I let it out, my eyes pinned to his. "I really like you too, Sawyer.

With that, he eases inside of me, stretching my body until I can't think anymore. I'm climbing all over again, and he moves a hand down, dragging one finger over me to keep time with his thrusts—my mind blessedly empty, and my heart hopelessly full.

Sawyer's pace quickens, and something about what's happening cracks my chest wide open. Every sweet gesture, every heated glance flooding my mind as my thoughts come rushing back to me. There's no time to pause and think about what's happening. All I know is that he is nothing like I thought he was.

Sawyer is thoughtful. Kind. He cares about his family and his job. I don't want any of this to end. Not just the sex, but this—him and me—us.

He groans into my mouth, his motions becoming erratic. It's enough to send me over the edge, and when we both finally break apart, gasping as we come down from the high, I'm certain of one very important detail:

I really, *really* like him.

TWENTY-SEVEN

Sawyer

I'm staring up at the ceiling of our hotel room, replaying the past six days over and over.

My palms are on my stomach, and I can hear the water running where Georgia is getting ready.

Warren is about to get married, and I'm pretty sure I'd give up everything for the girl in the bathroom.

Fuck.

If I thought I was down bad before, I am now so thoroughly ruined. I don't know what to think. All I know is that I don't want this trip to end.

My phone vibrates, and I pick it up to read the message from my mom.

Mom: Emerson said you never sent photos of your trip! She really wishes she could be there.

I smirk, shaking my head at the message. That

asshole got Mom on her side. Ruthless.

I scroll through my phone, looking at the photos I've taken. Georgia is in most of them, and I'm struggling to find enough to send to my family without alerting them to whatever is going on between us.

The door clicks open, and I sit up.

The dress.

Damn.

"I hope you don't like that outfit."

Georgia looks down at the emerald green dress, satin fabric clinging to her in all the right places—the places I've touched—kissed. "What's wrong with it?" She looks somewhat panicked. "Is it not dressy enough? Emerson said this would be fine."

I stand up, heat washing over me as I make my way in front of her, my hand migrating to her waist to feel the smooth material. "It's perfect," I whisper. "And I really want to take it off."

Georgia deadpans, her face unamused. "Very funny, but we are already late." She stretches to her toes to kiss my cheek and walks to her bags, pulling out a pair of heels.

"Emerson is asking for photos," I say, running my palm down my white button-up shirt. "Most of mine have you in them. Can you send me some neutral ones you've taken?"

"Sorry," Georgia's tone is mocking. "I already sent her mine. I guess that means I'm a better friend than you are a brother."

"Hey," I point a finger at her. "Take it back. I've known her longer."

Georgia huffs a laugh, bending down to fasten the strap of her shoe. When she stands up, a broad smile splits her face. "Ready?" she says.

I grab her hand, kissing her temple before leading her out the door.

The guys from the arcade are already sitting in the chairs lining the aisle when we enter the room where the wedding is being held. Chandeliers hang from the ceiling, and flowers line the white runner that stops at the altar.

Georgia and I take our seats somewhere in the middle as music floats through the air.

During the rehearsal dinner, we were able to take stock of the limited number of guests in attendance. Most of the faces look familiar, but I wouldn't be able to recall names if someone had a gun pointed to my head.

The only thing I can seem to think of is the girl sitting next to me.

I lean over to whisper to Georgia. "How long do you think this shit will take?"

She chuckles, smacking my arm gently. "This is your friend's wedding. Shouldn't you be a little more—" She waves her hands in the air. "Supportive?"

"I can be supportive while admitting that the ceremony is bound to be incredibly boring. Don't you think?" My eyes linger on her profile. Her hair is pulled back at the base of her neck, strands framing her face. I reach out and brush one to the side. "We go home in a few days."

Georgia exhales. "Yeah." Her eyes are on mine, my knuckles still brushing her cheek. "Ready to get rid of me?"

"No." I lean down to kiss her as the music starts

playing. Before I know it, Warren is up at the altar, looking more nervous than the time we got busted for sneaking out of his parents' house to go for a midnight swim in the creek with a few girls.

Distant memories.

As soon as Sadie walks in, the tension leaves his shoulders, and I can't help but smile. Georgia places her hand on my knee, and when I look over to see her expression, I'm not sure I ever want to get rid of her.

Not at all.

~

"Could they have picked a longer song for their first dance?" I'm taking a sip of water, my knee bouncing beneath our table.

Georgia's legs are crossed, her eyes watching Sadie and Warren retreat to their assigned seats, stopping to talk to people on the way.

"It *was* kind of long," she admits. "I can't imagine having my family stare at me like that."

"Friends, too," I say. Another slow song plays, and Sadie's parents are up, dancing at the center of the room first.

"We should do it." I gesture to where Kristin and Nash are now joining them. "You and me."

Georgia glances toward me, her eyes highlighted by the color of her dress. She huffs out a breath, her nose crinkling. "No," she says.

"Oh, come on." Something in the way her eyes flick over to the couples dancing tells me she isn't as opposed as

224

she says, and to be honest, I want to dance with her. I want to experience everything with her—show her off.

I stand up, offering her my hand. "You're supposed to be my date," I say. I clear my throat, deepening my voice. "Do you just find your partner barely tolerable?"

She laughs, grabbing my hand and standing, so I can lead us to the dance floor.

When my hands hit her waist, I pull her closer, remembering exactly how close we were the other night. I never want to stop getting closer—learning about her.

"You're going to be so jet-lagged when we get back," I whisper, a small smile on my face. "Whatever will you do? I won't be able to keep my toddler well-fed and well-rested."

"Shut up," she says. "I'm perfectly capable of feeding myself and taking a nap on my own."

"Damn." I lean down until my lips brush the side of her cheek, then slide them until my mouth is hovering near her ear. "I was eager to share a bed with you again."

She shudders, her fingers tangling through my hair gently as my grip on her tightens. Every touch from her has my body lighting up. Every word from her mouth has me begging for more.

"You're welcome to come over when we get back," she says. I can feel her smile against my cheek. "Though Emerson might be opposed to us fucking in her own home."

I chuckle, moving my hand just a hair lower. "You can come to my place, then. I'll make you a peanut butter and jelly, and we can play that game of *Twister*."

"Sounds like my kind of night." Her head is on my chest now.

"Of course, it does."

The music stops, and I'm left staring. She's so beautiful; I can't imagine why I ever saw anything else in her.

"You ready to leave?" I ask.

Georgia bites her lip, looking up at me from where she's standing. "Now's as good a time as any."

TWENTY-EIGHT

Georgia

I'm staring at a toaster, coils red and illuminated in the dim kitchen light of my apartment.

Sawyer and I got in late last night—really late. One delayed flight, and now I'm staring at a smoking toaster like a zombie from the latest hit television show.

Smoking? *Smoking.*

I slam my thumb against the cancel button, watching my hopes and dreams disintegrate the same way the blackened piece of toast is about to.

My arms are on the counter, and I lean down, planting my head on them and closing my eyes.

It's so nice down here. It really is. I could sleep forever—just like this—leaned over my kitchen countertop with my head on my forearms and my eyes closed. This would be the perfect way to fall asleep, and I wouldn't have to worry about teaching a class today. I could just fall into a dark abyss where I dream of glittering towers in the night, slow dancing, sharing headphones on an airplane, and feeling Sawyer's arms wrapped around my waist.

"I'm sorry I missed you last night." Emerson strides into the galley kitchen as my head pops up, my eyes opening. She drops her backpack, adjusting her oversized jean jacket. "Your flight got in really late, Georgia. Are you sure you're going to be ready to teach today?"

I yawn.

Which isn't exactly convincing.

"I have to get back to the real world sometime." I sigh as I stare at my burnt toast. "And then there's dinner with you, your parents, and Sawyer tonight."

Sawyer and I agreed we would just—bring it up. I don't really know how that is supposed to work, and we didn't necessarily come up with a plan. I'm not sure how Emerson is going to react.

Hey, I went to Paris with your brother, and we pretended to date. One thing led to another. We fucked, and now he's my boyfriend. I hope you don't mind.

I wince.

Yikes.

Emerson looks at my burnt piece of toast and winces before grabbing an apple off the countertop. She takes a bite and leaps onto the countertop. "You can just take a nap on the couch in the living room," she says. The smirk that stretches across her face is devious. "Won't you just love that—sleeping so close to my brother again?"

My cheeks are red. I can feel it like one of those hand boilers in science class. The thing that you hold onto so the heat of your hand makes the liquid rise and bubble? That's what's happening to my face. The room feels too hot.

"Wait." Emerson hops down off the counter, and her face twists into an expression I've never seen before. Realization, disgust, confusion, doubt. I have no idea. "What is that face for?"

"Nothing."

Not now. Please, not now.

"Georgia."

My phone buzzes on the counter next to the toaster, illuminating not only a text from my best friend's brother but also highlighting the lovely lock screen photo of Sawyer kissing my cheek.

Shit. Shit. Shit.

Emerson's eyes flick to the screen. "What the fuck is that?" She grabs the phone, holding it in front of her face and staring at the picture like a deer in the headlights.

I shrug. "Surprise." Oh yeah. I'm definitely cringing.

"You didn't," she says, putting my phone back down on the counter with a little too much force.

I jolt at the noise.

God, I'm tired.

I clear my throat. "About dinner tonight," I start. "We had something we were going to talk about."

Emerson punctuates the next three words. "Oh. My. God." Her jaw is practically on the floor as she takes one more look at the phone. "Georgia." Her voice is eerily quiet. "You fucked my brother, didn't you?"

Oof.

When she phrases it like that, it sounds so—

"I—"

"Shut up!" She's pointing at me now. "You did! You totally did!" Emerson places her hands on the counter behind her like she's going to fall over, and the relief washes over me at the smile that crosses her face. "I'm so sorry. I bet he's incredibly small. How unsatisfying."

He is . . . not.

She quickly holds a hand up and acts like she's gagging. "Oh, that was a bad joke." Emerson's nose wrinkles. "I don't want to know *anything*. Nothing at all. Please don't tell me."

I'm still trying to figure out what she's feeling—fighting through the hazy exhaustion weighing heavy on my bones. "Are you—" My brows furrow. "Upset?"

"Upset?" Emerson repeats. "No, no. I'm not upset. Confused? Fuck yeah."

"It just—"

She interrupts before I get the word out. "Please don't finish that sentence with the word *happened*." She takes another bite of her apple, mentally processing as she stares at the fridge. "Holy shit," she says. Emerson pulls her own phone out of her back pocket. "Oh my god, I have to go." She grabs her backpack off the floor and bolts to the door.

I step out of the kitchen to watch her leave.

"So, you're dating, right? Not just fucking." She looks almost pained.

"We're dating," I confirm.

"Well," she starts, her hand resting on the doorknob. "I'll process this all today while disassociating during one of my lame marketing classes." She bites the apple again and doesn't finish chewing before she speaks. "We can talk about it later, but Georgia?"

"Yeah?" I say.

Emerson tilts her head to the side, her features softening. "Are you happy?"

I nod, folding my arms across my chest.

It's not a lie—not in the slightest.

"Then I'm happy," Emerson says, slowly snaking her way out the door. Her head is the only part of her remaining in the apartment. "You can come to all the family dinners now."

A smile takes over my face. This went better than I imagined, though I never really imagined it going poorly. Emerson can be opinionated, but that never gets in the way of her being a good friend. There aren't a lot of good people in the world, and Emerson is good people. I can't imagine a better roommate.

"Love you, E," I say.

"Ew, you sap!" The door slams closed but quickly opens again, and her black hair is poking into the living room once more. "But I love you too, anyway." The door closes, and I chuckle, picking up my phone to check the message Sawyer left for me.

Sawyer: Ready for tonight?

Georgia: Funny story. Lol. Emerson is smart. A great detective, really.

Sawyer: She found out. Didn't she?

Georgia: Oops.

TWENTY-NINE

Sawyer

For some reason, I miss trying to order Georgia's coffee with copious amounts of pointing and over-exaggerated head nods.

Something about how fast and easy the process is now that we're home doesn't hit right. Though, it could be a good thing, since I'm barely standing up right now.

I press the buzzer to Rosewood High School, explaining that I'm bringing coffee to one of the student teachers, and they let me in with no questions asked.

The secretary smiles when I get to the counter to sign the visitor sign-in sheet.

"I remember you," she says, leaning her elbows on the desk behind the glass. "You stopped in a few weeks ago."

I smile, scribbling my name down in the tiny box. "That was me."

The secretary's eyes narrow. "Are you dating Miss

Clark?"

Well, someone doesn't beat around the bush.

She is all smiles when I look up. "Miss Clark is one of the good ones—stops in the office to chat frequently. It's nice to see that she has someone so handsome."

Oh, awkward.

I fight the urge to wince and mutter a *thanks* before picking up the two coffees. I think I do a decent job of plastering the smile to my face, so she doesn't find me rude.

"Tell her she should stop in during lunch."

I nod once. "Will do."

The hallways are empty since class already started, and I struggle to remember exactly where Georgia's classroom is supposed to be. I know it's on the first floor, but the last time I was here, someone showed me how to get there. Now, just after nine in the morning, I'm on my own and convinced they renovated the entire building and changed everything around overnight.

I think I get turned around at least three times before a kid comes striding out of the bathroom. "You here for Miss C.?" he asks, rolling the sleeves of his flannel down.

"Clark," I say, registering what he said. "Yeah, Miss Clark. Environmental Science."

"I was just headed back to class. I'll walk with you."

"Thanks." I nod, following the kid down the hallway. His dark eyes flick over his shoulder briefly, checking that I'm still behind him before he starts talking.

"So," he starts. "You're dating Miss C." The kid smiles, white teeth flashing as he runs a dark hand over his cropped hair.

"That seems to be the most common question in this school," I mutter. "Yeah, I'm dating her."

"She's probably one of my favorite teachers." He slows down, so I'm walking beside him. "I know what you're thinking, and it's nothing like that." The smile drops from his face, and I arch a tired brow. I wouldn't be surprised it if *was* like that, though. I've seen all of her. She's hot—also something I would have noticed in high school. "She's nice, has good jokes, and is always willing to help." He clears his throat. "Miss C. actually believes in us."

Well, holy shit.

High praise from a high school student. I don't think I remember a single high school teacher from when I was growing up. Georgia must leave a pretty good impression. I'm not surprised. She loves what she does, and she loves the kids more.

"She does care," I offer. "She talks about her students a lot."

"Yeah?" he says, his face lighting up. "She mentioned me, then. Probably told you about my good looks." He nudges my shoulder, and a chuckle breaks free. "I'm Miles," he says, stopping by the closed, wooden door.

My tired brain recognizes the name, recalling my time with Georgia over breakfast. "Oh, yeah. You're the one that's interested in ecology. You think about doing anything with that?"

He shrugs. "I don't know, probably." He puts his hand on the doorknob, turning it slowly. "I just turned seventeen, so I've got a year. It could be fun to study animals. Mrs. King lets me feed the snake sometimes."

"And Mrs. King is—"

"The teacher over Miss Clark." The smile breaks his face again. "You better start paying attention to your girlfriend, my man. Mine would shove me off a cliff if I forgot even the smallest detail about her life."

I laugh again as the door opens. "Noted."

Miles tosses a thumb over his shoulder to point at me before making his way to his seat.

Georgia stands at the white-board, and I'm trying so hard not to laugh at her. She has on the most ridiculous rubber overalls I've ever seen, with her hair piled in a messy bun atop her head. The giant net she's holding looks like she's about to catch a shark in the middle of the classroom.

"I brought you coffee," I say.

"Ow, ow! Miss Clark!" one of the female students shouts out, and Georgia gives her a death glare.

"Give me one second, guys." Georgia leans the net against the counter at the front of the classroom, and her rubber overalls squeak as she walks toward me.

I can't help but smile, my eyes skimming over her interesting uniform. "Nice get up," I say.

"They're chest waders." She tilts her head, looking at me like *I'm* the idiot, and something about the way she does it has me agreeing.

Anything she asks.

"I got you coffee since I figured you'd be tired."

She grabs the cup out of my hand and pops the lid off, blowing on the steaming liquid before taking a sip and setting it on the counter. "I have to get back to teaching," she says quietly.

The class has erupted in soft murmurs, and I have to admit that having twenty-some teenagers staring at you is pretty intimidating. "That's fine," I say.

"We are going creeking in about five minutes to catch some crawdads and do some water quality testing." She looks back at the teacher in the back of the room, the same one that was here before.

I wave, and Mrs. King, I assume, smiles at me. "Sounds fun," I say. "So, Emerson. Is she good?"

Georgia sighs. "Yeah, she's fine. Shocked, obviously." She tugs at a stray strand of hair that fell out of her bun and wraps it up with the rest, tucking it—wherever. "I really do have to go, though." She smiles. "Thank you for the coffee." Her voice drops to a whisper. "I can't really kiss you here, but just know; I definitely want to."

I rub the back of my neck, my pulse quickening at the thought. "Don't worry," I say. "I'd rather you just stand here thinking about it for the rest of the day, anyway." I lean in, just a hair, dropping my voice so her students can't hear. "It'll make whatever we do after dinner far more enjoyable. The anticipation." I waggle my eyebrows and notice the way her cheeks turn a shade of pink.

"Okay," she says, turning to look out at the class. "I think I'm going to ride with Emerson, so I'll just meet you at your parents' house."

"Of course." I'm backing up toward the door with my own coffee in hand. "Hopefully we can stay awake long enough for *game night* after dinner."

Georgia smiles before taking another sip of her coffee. "Hopefully," she responds.

And just like that, I'm walking back through the hallways, trying to remember every turn Miles took on the way in and trying not to picture Georgia stripped down and playing that game of *Twister*.

I rub my hand down my face.

This time, she's definitely on top.

THIRTY

Georgia

"You already told your parents?"

Emerson pulls into the driveway as I play with a stray thread on the side of my overalls. I'm nervous, and I know it's for no reason. I already know Sandra and Henry from the times I've spent with them over breaks—the ones I couldn't afford to go home for. It's not like I'm meeting them for the first time—but still.

"Nah." Emerson puts the car in park. "That's all you and Sawyer." She glances in the rearview mirror. "Speaking of."

Sawyer pulls in beside us, parks, and jumps out to open my door. "Long time no see," he says, pulling me to his chest.

That lemongrass scent invades my lungs, and I realize it probably wasn't the soap at the hotel. I think he just smells like that.

It's my new favorite scent.

"Yeah," Emerson says, closing the door on the other side of her car. "This is a little weird."

Sawyer cocks an eyebrow at his sister, moving forward until my back hits the car and his lips are on mine.

"Oh, gross." I can hear Emerson walking up to the door, gagging. "I'm fine with you two together, but seriously, stop."

Breaking the kiss, Sawyer grabs my hand, lacing his fingers through mine as he drags me into the house.

"That was not necessary," I whisper.

"I didn't get to kiss you at school," he says. "I was just making up for it."

"In front of Emerson?" She's already disappeared inside—practically ran. We should have timed her. We'd be rich.

He shrugs, looking rather pleased with himself. "That was just to piss her off. She's funny when she's angry."

I laugh, shaking my head when we reach the steps to the porch. "You're such an asshole."

Emerson opens the door, and I let go of Sawyer's hand, suddenly wrapped in a warm hug as Sandra greets us.

"You're back," she says, beaming at Sawyer.

"Yeah, Ma." Sawyer kisses his mom on the temple before pulling his shoes off. "And before you ask, it was fun."

"How are you, Georgia?" Sandra's hands are on my shoulders as she looks me over, her brown eyes taking me in. "It's been a while since we've seen you. I was surprised when Emerson said you were going on the trip with Sawyer."

I can feel the blush creep up my neck, warming my cheeks as I look away. "Me too." I clear my throat.

Emerson already retreated to the kitchen—probably leaning on that same counter that held Sawyer's ridiculous cookies—the ones I threw in the trash.

Funny.

"Well, come on in," Sandra says, wiping her hands on her apron before brushing black strands of hair behind her shoulder. "Food's almost ready."

I catch Sawyer looking at me before following his mom into the kitchen where Henry stands over the stove, dipping a spoon into whatever pasta sauce was cooking before shoving it into his mouth.

"Henry, that better be the first time that spoon touched my food." Sandra's sharp voice cuts through the air.

Henry's eyes widen before he tosses the spoon in the sink and looks back at me. "She sure is scary," he says before turning to his wife. "I would never taint your cooking, dear. I like my head firmly attached to my neck."

Emerson laughs from where her elbows are resting on the counter, and I briefly feel Sawyer grab the fabric of my overalls at my back—just briefly.

I turn back, the smirk breaking across my face. He returns the expression, and when I look back at Sandra, her eyes are narrowed.

"So, the trip was good? Yes?" she questions.

"I already answered that," Sawyer groans, shoving his hands in his pocket.

"I want to hear from Georgia."

My heart pounds in my chest, and I'm pretty sure I'm

sweating. I'm definitely sweating. In fact, pretty soon, there will be a puddle beneath my feet, and I'll be kicked out of the home for ruining the hardwood.

"It was great," I say, trying to plaster a natural-looking smile on my face.

"Hm." Sawyer's mom turns, tending to whatever food is making the house smell so damn delicious.

I didn't realize how hungry I was, but I assume I should have known. Shoving fruit snacks and pretzels in your face for ten minutes isn't exactly a lunch.

I'm surprised I'm still walking.

"Well," Sandra starts, "You guys can sit down if you want. The dining room is set, and I'm hungry. For the sake of being a good host, I refuse to eat first, so I ask that you all hurry."

Henry kisses his wife before leading the way to the dining room, where I go to sit at the wooden table. Sawyer is next to me in an instant, and Emerson finds her way across from us, a smug look on her face.

Once everyone is seated, silence stretches across the room, and I can't help the way my nerves are skating through my body.

What is wrong with me?

"So, Ma," Sawyer says, breaking the silence. I quickly take a bite of pasta and try to fight the way my stomach is now suddenly in my throat. "Funny story."

Sandra waves a hand, dismissing him. "You don't have to say anything." She picks up her drink and takes a sip before continuing. "You two are together. I have eyes, Son."

Sawyer narrows his gaze at Emerson, who is on the

verge of cracking up. "You're a traitor, Nemo."

That's when Emerson lets out a real laugh. "It wasn't me," she says. "I swear it."

"Honestly, Sawyer," his mom cuts in. "Nobody had to tell me." She smiles from the head of the table, looking at me like she couldn't be more pleased. All of those nerves wash out of me in an instant, and I feel a little more normal. "Glad to keep you close to the family, Georgia. You already know we love you."

Henry sets down a fork, looking somewhat confused. "Wait, back up," he says. "What?"

I laugh at the annoyed expression his wife gives him before Sawyer jumps in to explain. "Dad, we're dating."

"You and Georgia?" he says, eyes flicking between us. "Yikes. How did that happen?"

"What do you mean, *yikes,* Henry?" Sandra's brown eyes throw daggers.

Sawyer's dad raises his hands in defense. "Last I heard, Emerson was worried about them murdering one another on their trip."

"That's definitely how it started," I say.

Henry looks at me again. "So, tell us about the trip." He takes a sip of his water. "Maybe not every detail, but the stuff we'd like to know."

Oh god.

No.

No. Absolutely not.

Emerson's groan is just as loud as my thoughts. "*Dad,*" she says.

"I'm *just* clarifying."

243

Sawyer's shoulders are shaking with the laughter that is now taking over his body, leaving me to explain the parts of the trip I'm willing to share.

Sometime after our conversation about Paris, Sawyer's family starts talking about some new action movie that's coming out. Emerson and her dad want to go see it; Sandra is completely opposed.

That's when I feel Sawyer's hand migrate to my thigh, just above my knee as he mentions wanting to see the movie, too. I have no idea what movie it is—not when he squeezes gently, and certainly not when his hand rises slowly, that one touch feeling like a thousand suns.

He leans in as the conversation continues around us. "What are you thinking about?" he asks, his thumb stroking over the fabric of my clothes, his lips close to me. It's unbearable.

"Game night," I supply.

Sawyer squeezes my thigh again—harder—and I'm pretty sure I'm about to combust. My stomach is curling and twisting in a way that has my mind going blank.

I clear my throat. "How does Friday sound for a game night? I can buy Candyland."

"Candyland is boring." The corner of Sawyer's mouth lifts—just slightly. I *cannot* be looking at his mouth right now. "You'll have to think of something else."

My heart is thrashing in my chest, my mind dizzy. "I think I can come up with something."

Emerson's eyes narrow at us from across the table, and I quickly brush Sawyer's hand away from me before speaking.

"So, Sandra," I start as Sawyer picks up his glass of water and takes a drink. "I never asked about the pug decorations in the bathroom. Where did you get them?"

Sawyer practically chokes on his drink, laughing as Sandra tells me about her favorite places to shop online.

I don't hear much of it, though.

Not when my mind can only think about what could possibly happen on Friday.

THIRTY-ONE

Sawyer

Leo left early Friday morning, leaving me to run the kitchen on my own, and even though I was busting my ass the entire time, I can't say I didn't enjoy it.

I've been thinking about what I told Georgia a lot lately, and with Leo's new desire to travel with his husband, I'm getting more of a taste for running my own kitchen.

And wondering what it might be like to run my own restaurant.

When I get back to my apartment, I throw my keys on the kitchen table, grab ingredients from the cabinet, and set them out. Georgia should be here soon, and even though I know she doesn't cook much, I *do* know the girl loves a good competition.

A knock on my door draws my attention as I finish setting everything up.

My heart is racing, and I can't say I'm not excited to

see her. After dinner with my parents, things got pretty busy at Catch 45, and Georgia's been grinding away trying to finish her final project for student teaching. I guess it's some huge presentation.

She kept going on about data, assessments, formative and summative—something. I have no idea, but she can't wait to have her own classroom. That much I picked up on.

"Hey," I say, opening the door.

Georgia is leaning down, fixing the cuff at the bottom of her jeans before grabbing the grocery bag off the floor.

"What did you bring?" I ask.

"It's game night, remember?" She moves past me, setting the bag on the coffee table and looking around my apartment.

It's the first time she's been here, but I can't seem to focus on anything aside from the words *game night*, and the way her cropped, white shirt reveals a small patch of skin.

Skin that I want to be touching.

It's been a while since I've been able to touch her.

"So, uh—" I dodge the couch and move to stand in front of her, nervously rubbing the back of my neck. "I thought you'd be up for a little competition." I smile. "Of the cooking variety."

Her brows furrow, and she tugs on the thick braid hanging over one shoulder. "What kind of cooking competition?"

I shrug, suddenly doubting my idea. At the time, it seemed like fun, but now I'm not so sure. "I figured we could see who can come up with the better pancake recipe. I bought a bunch of shit for it. It's all set out in the kitchen."

A slow smile spreads across her face as her eyes flick behind me. "Oh, yes." Georgia kisses my cheek, moving around me to find the kitchen. "You're going down Chef Owens."

I laugh, following her as I explain what I had in mind.

~

"Here you are," Georgia says, setting her plate on the kitchen table. "Peanut butter and jelly pancakes."

I grab my own dish from the counter, dropping it in front of where she stands. "And here *you* are."

Georgia groans when she looks at the plate. "Why does yours look so fancy?" She leans against the table, glaring at my pancakes as if they have personally offended her. "Okay, Chef Owens. What did you make?"

I smile, hoping that leaning into more of a dessert was the right option. "S'mores," I say.

Georgia turns to face me, squaring her stance and leveling her gaze. She folds her arms across her chest and glares at me like I am now the new offending party. "To be fair," she starts. "We both made toddler food."

I laugh, leaning down to kiss her, my hand tugging her closer by the waist. "I guess so," I say, my mouth inches from hers. The smell of pears and the smallest hint of mint linger on her breath.

When she runs her fingers through my hair, tugging gently as she presses her mouth back to mine, a dark rumble runs through my throat. My entire body is alight with whatever intoxicating spell Georgia has put me under.

I can't say I don't enjoy it.

I pull back, my fingers still digging into her sides and desperate for more contact. "Eat first, then we can play your game." My voice is raspy, laced with desire. "What game did you bring, by the way?"

She smiles, slipping her hand beneath my t-shirt and tracing the waistband of my jeans. I hiss at the contact, my mind going blank.

Fuck.

"I think you know," she whispers before turning around to sit in front of the meal I made. "Looks good," she says. "But I'm wondering if your pancakes belong in the trash—just like your cookies."

I point at her, barely able to hold back my grin. "That's a low blow," I say.

"No, it's not." Georgia is grabbing a fork and cutting into one of my pancakes with the side. "But I'd be happy to show you one of those later."

My mouth is hanging open, and if I wasn't hard before, I could now give a diamond a run for its money.

Fucking hell.

~

"This is just making me realize how old I am," I groan, trying to hold my body up in a never-ending plank.

This game sounded a lot hotter when we were talking about it. Now, it just seems like Georgia became my gym buddy, and we are working to beat the world record for the longest plank ever held. I could be considered a skilled warrior in a fantasy novel at this point. I'm pretty sure it's been longer than five minutes.

"Right foot, red," Georgia says, a smug smirk on her face.

It's a little rude, considering she's hanging out in downward dog.

Her ass looks nice, though.

I try to twist around, looking for an empty dot to place my foot on, realizing that my arms are shaking.

As soon as I lift up, my limbs give out, and I collapse to the ground. Georgia lets out the most heinous cackle, standing up and looking down at me as I roll onto my back.

I still can't wipe the smile off my face.

"I won!" She kneels, swinging one leg over my torso until she's straddling me. "I didn't even have to cheat."

I swallow, my thoughts suddenly leaving my skull as I look up at her. "Right," I rasp, my fingers landing on her hips.

All I know is that she's right there—against me.

Georgia's hazel eyes intensify, blazing greener as her lips part. I don't think I've wanted anything more in my life.

I want her—all of her—just as she is. I can't seem to get enough. We've texted nonstop since returning to the states, and I can't help but thinking I want to live the rest of my life talking to her—being with her.

It's out of control.

"Done playing?" I ask.

Georgia nods, leaning down until her mouth is hovering over mine. "You never gave me the tour," she whispers. "I didn't get to see your bedroom."

"It's probably better than the king's quarters in the palace of Versailles."

"Oh, really?"

"Of course."

Georgia pushes off my chest and stands up. I'm helpless to follow, grabbing her hand and taking the lead as I drag her down the hallway to my bedroom.

"Oh nice," she says, trailing her fingers over the wooden surface of my dresser.

I move to stand behind her, noticing the way she sucks in a breath as I lean down. My lips brush her neck and sparks shoot across my flesh. I pull her closer until her body is against mine, desperate for more contact—more of *her*.

"I keep imagining you in those ridiculous rubber overalls," I whisper, and Georgia chuckles, the sound airy as she tilts her head to the side. I take the opportunity and press another kiss to her flushed skin.

"They are exceptionally flattering," she says.

My lips are trailing down her neck, gently carving a path that has my pulse spiking and her breathing shallow. "I think I like them better off, though."

Georgia spins, her lips crashing into mine as her hands tug at my hair, dragging a groan from deep in my throat.

I fist the hem of her shirt and drag it over her head.

My eyes fall to the black bra she's wearing before I tug the fabric down, trailing hungry kisses over her collarbone and down to the swell of her breast. When my tongue flicks against her nipple, she whimpers, slowly backing up until her legs hit the bed.

Finally.

The next few moments are filled with harsh sounds and missing clothes as I trail my lips over every possible inch of her skin.

When she's finally beneath me, her fingers tracing over my pecs, I look down and take in the way her skin looks—her lips. Swollen and pink. When her gaze meets mine, my chest tightens.

Her fingers move steadily until they're dragging down my tensing stomach, ghosting over my sensitized flesh. Lower—lower.

She drags her hand down my length, and I hiss as pleasure shoots up my spine.

It's too much.

"Georgia." My voice is a warning, but she moves her hand again—again. All I can think about is friction as her hand works me.

"I made you a promise," she whispers.

I can't for the life of me remember what that promise might be.

My hips are moving, chasing all that she's giving me.

"Yeah?" My voice is low.

"I need you on your back, Sawyer."

Oh fuck.

Her hand is gone, and I'm left panting, rolling over until Georgia is on top of me, trailing her lips down my chest, my stomach—lower, still.

My eyes are on the ceiling, my heart is pounding. Is she going to—

Her mouth parts around me, and the entire world stops. I'm not going to last a minute with her like this. Not when her tongue drags up my hardened flesh, and my entire body is tensing up like a bomb about to detonate.

"Jesus Christ, Georgia. You have to stop."

Her chuckle vibrates in a way that has pleasure intensifying, and I know I'm about to end this before it even begins.

My fingers are in her hair, and she pulls back until her eyes meet mine—so painfully beautiful that I might die from her presence, alone.

"What do you want?" she asks, licking her lips and—

God damn.

"Ride me." I practically pant as she slowly moves up my body, her knees on either side of my hips.

When I feel her against me—grinding—I almost forget my own damn name.

Georgia reaches down, positioning me until she can slowly lower herself.

It's too good.

Way too good.

I look down at where our bodies connect, moving my hand until my thumb gently strokes her, matching her motions.

Georgia moans, and I'm suddenly moving faster, lifting my hips to keep time with my strokes, working my fingers over her until the room fills with the sounds of our harsh breathing and slick skin.

Georgia keeps moving, and my hands run up her torso as she grinds herself against me—her mouth meeting mine and her tongue tracing over my lips in a way that has me starving.

"I'm—*fuck*." I can't get a word out. Everything is building, and there's literally nothing I could think of that would stop where this is going. "Are you close?" I ask.

Georgia nods, releasing a shuddering breath, her legs beginning to shake.

And with that, we both go over the edge.

When we break apart, my chest cracks open so thoroughly that I'm pretty sure Georgia Clark has ruined me for anyone else.

Her head drops to the crook of my neck, her breathing settling, and I skim my fingertips over her back, relishing in the feel of her soft skin.

"You know," I say. "I think, in the end, you really were the winner."

Georgia laughs, her breath fanning over my chest. "I never doubted that for a second."

THIRTY-TWO

Georgia

When the light floats over me from the window, I'm taken back to Paris.

Sawyer is sprawled out on his stomach, his breathing steady as the coming morning. I look over at his back, his arms stretched above his head.

My chest tightens—that warm feeling overtaking me as I stare at the man I used to hate with every ounce of my being. It's hard to remember why, or what made my distaste so strong.

I drag myself off the bed, finding his t-shirt discarded on the floor. I pull the fabric over my head, tugging it down until it kisses the middle of my thighs.

My hair is a tangled mess, but I don't bother with it as I walk out to the kitchen, searching the cabinets for any source of caffeine. I know Sawyer drinks coffee because he did when we were in Paris and brought his own cup to school. The only question is, where the hell does he keep it?

When I find the coffee beans, I notice that they aren't ground, and it takes me about twenty minutes of fidgeting with his fancy coffee pot before I figure out how to make one simple cup of coffee.

I huff a laugh while pouring the liquid into a mug I found.

"Sous chef," I mutter. "He *would* have a coffee pot like this."

Doesn't he know that caffeine is a drug, and as an addict myself, this process is entirely too complex? I need my hit faster.

My phone buzzes from where I left it on the counter, the screen lighting up with a picture of Emerson during a drunken night of karaoke from a few months ago. Every time I see the picture when she calls me, I'm reminded that even drunk, Emerson is a great singer.

I, however, sound like a dying walrus.

I pick up the phone, sliding my finger across the screen to answer and something stirs in my gut—a nagging sensation that has warning bells ringing.

"Hello?"

She's crying.

Emerson never cries.

"Georgia?"

My hands are trembling as the entire world seems to stop spinning. That feeling in my gut festers and swells until I'm consumed by a dread so thick, it feels like I'm standing in a vat of glue, unable to move from my spot in the kitchen.

Emerson's voice shakes. "I've been trying to get

ahold of Sawyer, but I think his phone is dead." I hear her sniff, and something cracks in my chest. "It just keeps going to voicemail."

I'm waiting for her to continue—frozen.

"It's Mom, Georgia."

The earth stops spinning.

"What happened?" My voice is strained—barely a whisper. I don't like crying, and I hate the stinging feeling as tears well up in my eyes. But no amount of gripping Sawyer's counter can chase them away.

This isn't right.

"There was an accident late last night," Emerson starts. The pain in her voice tears a hole right through me as I feel moisture slide down my cheek.

I'm walking back to the bedroom, dreading what is going to happen when I wake Sawyer up—when I have to explain.

"She's at Riverview hospital," Emerson squeaks out before she gasps, fighting for breath. My tears are flowing steadily at this point, and all I can think about is Sandra during our dinner on Monday, kind and warm—here. "She's in critical. I guess some kid was driving and hit her car head on. They think he had been drinking."

I try to keep my voice steady. The last thing Emerson needs is my own emotions clouding my ability to be there for her—for Sawyer. She needs—shit—I don't know what she needs, but I'll be damned if I don't provide it.

"I'll get Sawyer," I say, pushing against the wooden door to the bedroom.

"Georgia," Emerson says on the end of the line. "Let

me tell him." There's a pause before she whispers, "Please."

"Of course."

The entire room feels like it's covered in a thick fog, one that's keeping me from feeling the depth of what's happening. My ears are ringing in the silence as I run my hand over Sawyer's back.

He sits up, taking in my expression before bolting upright.

I hold the phone out to him and watch as he listens to whatever Emerson is saying on the other end of the line.

He's still—eerily so.

His eyes are glazed over, and he looks like he's barely breathing.

I can't stop the tightness in my chest as he hangs up the phone, handing it to me slowly before whispering, "We have to go."

I nod, grabbing my clothes off the floor and making my way to the bathroom with my phone in my hand.

As I look in the mirror, some of that fog starts to break apart, and I can feel the pain creeping and crawling up my throat, begging me to scream—something—anything.

I wipe my hand across my cheek, smearing the dampness there before I pull on my clothes.

Checking my phone for any news articles, I find what I'm looking for. I don't know what I thought looking at the article would do. They haven't released the name of the teenager since he's a minor, but the article details the head-on collision.

Maybe I think reading it will make it less real—like reading the news this way will allow me to detach.

It'll be easier if I can detach—be there for Sawyer and Emerson—their family.

My phone buzzes, and I notice a missed text message from Lindsay King.

If pain were the weather, it would be a summer thunderstorm—rolling in slowly until lightning was flashing across the sky, burning the scorched earth just before the rain takes over and consumes.

I don't know what part of the storm I'm in now, but I can feel the electricity buzzing over my skin—like the lightning is about to strike—ruthless in its pursuit.

It's going to hit us, and it's going to hit hard.

Lindsay King: I tried to call you. Miles got into an accident last night. He's okay, but the other driver isn't doing well.

My knees are weak as the knock sounds just before Sawyer walks in. His face is pale, his body frozen like he's still in that same thick fog that keeps him from feeling whatever it is he's about to feel.

I try to hold in the sob building in my throat; the pain slicing two ways.

Miles.

"You ready?" he says, his tone cold—quiet.

I swallow the emotions, wrapping my arms around his waist and nodding before burying my face in his warm chest. Whatever happens, I need to suck it up. I cannot break apart. Not now.

"Yeah," I say as his arms wrap around me, barely

squeezing as if all strength has left him.

I want to be there for him.

I just don't know how.

"Let's go," I whisper.

THIRTY-THREE

Sawyer

I feel disconnected from my body. Even as the sterile scent of the hospital assaults my senses, I can't seem to register where I am—what is happening.

I've never heard Emerson cry like that.

I know she was trying to hide it—keep it together, but I could just *tell*.

She's breaking so thoroughly that I'm scared of what will happen when my own emotions catch up to me.

Georgia sits next to me, handing me a cup of coffee from the cafeteria, and leaning back in her chair. Her eyes are puffy and swollen, but I haven't seen any more tears leave, though sometimes when I look at her, those hazel eyes become glassy.

I think she's trying to be strong for my sake.

I hate that, too.

I take a sip of the steaming liquid, tasting the bitter

shit that is hospital coffee. It doesn't matter though—not now.

Emerson and Dad are back in the room, and we are waiting for a chance to go back there.

I'm not sure I want to know what I'll find.

What's worse is the hospital is restricting visitation to only family, so Georgia will be sitting out here.

Alone.

That fact makes me feel guilty, too.

"What kind of idiot," I mutter, dragging my hand down my face.

The more I think about what Emerson told me—the news article—the angrier I become. Some kid got behind the wheel of a car after drinking. I hope he suffers the consequences for the rest of his natural life.

I hang my head between my knees as Georgia's palm runs over my back. I know it's not right, but anger is the easy emotion—the safe one.

"That kid," I say before letting out a long breath. "I fucking hope this scars him."

Georgia flinches. It's barely there, but I feel it just before her palm is off my back. "You're angry," she says, her voice quiet.

I snap. "Of course, I'm angry." Pinching the bridge of my nose, I try like hell to hold on to that emotion. I don't know what lurks beneath it because I haven't been able to feel that yet. At least I know what to expect with my anger. I can sit here and blame the kid. Maybe then I'll feel like I have some ounce of control.

"How is it fair?" My voice cracks as I look back at

Georgia. Pain etches across her features—pain and exhaustion. It's not *fair* for me to make her carry this, but I don't know what else to do with it. "How is it that the one who fucked up is walking around fine? How is that fair?" I'm trembling, and I'm afraid my chest is going to crack open right open—bleeding out onto the white tile below.

Georgia's eyes turn glassy again. "He's just a kid, Sawyer."

"Whoever he is, he seems to be old enough to drink." My jaw feels tight as I clench my teeth together. "Or maybe he isn't. *Motherfucker.*"

It's just so easy to blame him—the faceless teenager that has my mom's life hanging in the balance.

"Sawyer." A stray tear skates down her cheek, and Georgia almost looks guilty that she let it go. Her tone is soft, just like the hand that is now resting against my arm. "He was one of mine." Her voice is so quiet I can barely hear her.

"What?"

"The teenager," she says as another bead of moisture collects in the corner of her eye. She dabs it away with the sleeve of her shirt. "He's one of my students."

Fuck.

Fuck.

My eyes trace over her features, trying to figure out what she's feeling—who she is feeling it for.

That's the part that starts to sting—the realization that I cannot logically expect Georgia to sit here and support me. I've heard her talk about her students. She loves them— I just don't think I can—

"Fuck." The word leaves my mouth on a breath as I

throw myself back in the chair.

I don't like the pain that's slowly creeping upward, so I tug on the anger. I let the rage drive me. "I hope he rots," I mutter.

Georgia flinches.

"You don't mean that," she says.

The anger builds, swelling in my chest until my emotions harden into something like armor—something impenetrable—something that will allow me to walk back into that fucking hospital room and not lose my shit. "I do."

"You're being irrational."

"Irrational." My eyes are blazing as they snap to her, the pain still written across her face. I can't bring myself to touch whatever twists in my chest at the way she's looking at me. I can't handle both things right now.

"Look, Sawyer," she says, leaning in. "I care." She swallows, mustering up the courage to say more. "I care a lot. I care about *both* of them."

It ignites something within me—something I don't fully understand. I can't focus when she's talking about this. My mind just keeps picturing a future, one without my mom. "Maybe you should leave," I whisper.

Georgia looks like she's been slapped. "Leave?"

"You can't come back, anyway. You're not family, and I really can't listen to you—" I hit the arm of the chair as Georgia jolts in her own seat. The guilt of that small movement is too much. I need to be alone. "Shit," I say. "I want you to leave."

"Really, Sawyer?" Her tone is soft, but what she said stings—deep. It's slicing through me, and I can feel all that pain welling to the surface. My armor doesn't stand a chance.

"Goddamn it, I need you to leave!" My voice is too loud, and a nurse looks over at me from behind the desk before muttering to her coworker.

I'm out of control, and I don't want Georgia around to watch me break apart.

"Please." I quiet myself, unsure if she even hears me.

Georgia gets up, draping her jacket over her arm, and I can't bear to look at her as she stands over me.

I'm pathetic.

Weak.

Crumbling.

"If that's what you want," she says. "If you really think I can't be here for you."

"That's what I want." The sentence burns on my tongue.

"Okay."

Georgia is walking away before I can think better of it, and that pain finally stabs through my heart. I can feel the stinging of tears when the doctor walks out, Emerson trailing behind with dark circles etched beneath her eyes. She looks like she hasn't slept in weeks.

I wrap her in my arms, trying to tell my own emotions to fuck off for the moment. "You good?" I ask.

"Yeah." She breaks away from my grip, wiping her nose with her sleeve. "Where's Georgia?"

"Gone," I say.

Emerson's brows furrow. "Oh, I—" She clears her throat. "I'll just call her. We shouldn't make her wait here, anyway. It's not fair if she can't go back."

"Mr. Owens," the doctor cuts in. "Your dad is waiting for you back in the room."

There's sympathy plastered on his face—the kind of mask he's probably used to wearing. It's the face doctors make when they know someone's loved one has a chance of dying.

My *mom* has a chance of dying.

That asshole kid is walking free.

"Right," I say. "I'm ready."

Somehow, I don't believe I am—not in the slightest. The only problem is that I have to be.

THIRTY-FOUR

Georgia

I don't know what to do.

If it wasn't obvious before, it's obvious now.

I stare at the text messages between me and Sawyer, trying to piece together the right things to say—the right things to do.

I've done none of them.

Georgia: I was wrong. Everything I said was wrong. I'm so sorry, Sawyer.

The bubbles appear, disappear, and reappear. Then they go away entirely, and I know I've fucked up again.

I can't even apologize correctly.

I'm drowning, and there's no use in feeling sorry for myself.

Lindsay sits at her desk at the back of the room,

quietly rustling through papers I barely managed to grade before this morning.

Emerson called me from the hospital to talk, and I just let her talk. I didn't say a single word. I think I was too afraid to.

Especially after what I said to Sawyer. It wasn't the time to defend Miles, but I'm walking through my own grief right now.

When Emerson came home on Saturday night, she looked like a ghost, crawling into my bed without a word before the sobs racked her body.

I didn't know what to do then either, so I just let her cry, lacing my fingers through hers and trying to keep my thoughts elsewhere.

If I were being honest—if I didn't feel guilty for the thoughts running through my mind, I wouldn't keep trying to block them out.

Sawyer had every right to be angry. There wasn't a second when I thought he shouldn't be, but at the same time—

I've spent this entire year getting to know these kids, and I felt like I needed to defend him.

I shouldn't have.

Miles fucked up.

When Emerson's hand squeezed mine, her breathing evening out in the darkness of my bedroom, I said the only thing I was certain wouldn't make things worse.

The thing that was true.

"I love you, E."

"I know, Georgia." Her hand tightened around mine.

"I know you do."

My phone vibrates in my palm, and I squeeze it tighter, seeing Sawyer's name finally pop up on the screen.

Sawyer: What you said was shitty.

I close my eyes, guilt wrapping around my heart like vines and squeezing so tight, I'm sure it will stop beating at any moment. There's too much grief—too much sadness. Sadness for the woman who opened her home to me when I couldn't make it home—sadness for the kid that showed me I could actually inspire people to do something with their lives.

Even then, that inspiration didn't work out.
Did it?

Sawyer: Emerson said she would stay at the house with me and Dad tonight. Please don't come over.

Fuck.

I have class in twenty minutes, and I'm not sure how things will be. Typically, when an accident happens in a school like this, the students know. They'll have opinions, and though the counselors open themselves up to chat, kids will want to chat with *me*. It's not like they know all the ways I was connected to this event.

They couldn't.

Lindsay already informed me that Miles won't be coming during the school day. He will probably be gone for a while.

I try to come up with something to say to Sawyer, wishing I could be what he needed, but I'm not—I wasn't, and I'm not sure I can be right now.

But I want to try.

Georgia: Whatever you need.

Even if that doesn't include me, I'll offer it.

A gentle knock sounds at the door before Miles walks into the classroom. His face is ashen as he leans against crutches.

"Miss C." His voice is trembling, and he looks like he expects me to hate him—to reprimand him. "I just came for my work."

Lindsay looks up over her wire-framed reading glasses, nodding toward me.

"Of course." I walk over to the counter at the front of the room, gathering the papers stacked there.

I tried to cut down on the work he would have to do, but somehow it still feels wrong to hand him a pile of academic worksheets after what happened.

I glance up, walking toward Miles and holding out the papers in my hand.

That's when he crumbles, and I can feel my chest cave in as I watch my student sob in front of me.

"I fucked up, Miss C."

I'm frozen—unsure of what to say. It's going to be wrong all over again, and I don't think I can hold my own tears back, so I let him talk.

"You believed in me," he confesses, his face twisting

the same way my heart is. "You're the first person to believe I could do something with my life—anything I imagined, and I went and destroyed it."

My eyes sting, and all I can feel is the immense pressure of *hurt*. It isn't even my hurt to have, but it's there—nagging and incessant. "Miles," I whisper.

I set the papers down on the counter, trying to figure out what to do. There was no training on this—no class that could help me navigate this terrain.

Miles is shaking, and I reach out, placing my hand on his shoulder and desperately hoping for—something.

I can't fix this.

"I shouldn't even be crying," he says. "That woman I hit—"

The tears are rolling down my cheeks, and I can feel them as they cut their path, salt coating my lips. "Miles," I whisper, trying desperately to communicate something right—something good. "We all mess up." It sounds so lame—trivial. "Everyone has made ridiculous, horrible mistakes. There isn't a soul on this earth who doesn't deserve blame."

He's still crying.

I take a deep breath.

"We are responsible for the consequences, no matter what those are, but you have to know—please know." I'm fighting to keep the sobs from taking over—fighting the way my voice shakes. "I do not love any of my students less because they make mistakes." I squeeze his shoulder gently. "I spend a lot of time judging based on merit, but you have to know that I do not judge you right now."

I don't know if there are words enough to express what I'm feeling. Everything feels wrong and disjointed.

Miles swipes a hand over his eyes. "I don't deserve forgiveness."

"Honey, nobody does." I'm shaking my head, trying desperately to keep myself together. "Nobody does, and yet it's given, anyway."

As Miles glances at the clock, he picks up the papers. "I have to go."

My hand drops away, and with that, he's gone.

Lindsay walks up to me, leaning against the counter. Her eyes glassy as she places a warm hand over mine.

I can't stop sobbing.

"And that's why we do it." She offers a wan smile. "Hearts go on breaking, but it's a lot easier when there's someone by your side."

"I didn't say the right thing." I feel weak—*stupid.*

"There isn't anything right to say," she says, patting my hand. "But you didn't look at that boy with disgust. You didn't condemn him, and that speaks more than the words ever could."

I nod, wiping my face as Lindsay walks to the board.

"Go home, Georgia. I think I can handle my own classroom for one day."

"My lessons—"

"Are nothing I can't teach." Lindsay wraps me in her arms, and I can't for the life of me figure out why I needed that so much.

"Thank you," I whisper.

She nods silently as I grab my bag, shrugging it over

my shoulder and forcing myself to trudge down the hallway despite the heaviness weighing in the air.

THIRTY-FIVE

Sawyer

I don't feel anything.

The television glows in the darkened room at my parents' house. The beer bottle in my hand isn't cold anymore.

I don't usually drink—but I thought it might take the edge off.

It didn't.

My mind keeps replaying everything that happened in the hospital. I try not to picture my mom, but that doesn't stop the images from coming back up.

And then there's Georgia.

I know exactly what my mother would say about that situation—how she is. She would remind me that Georgia is being pulled in a thousand different directions, and I should have compassion.

I run my hand down my face, pulling up our text

messages again.

Georgia: Whatever you need.

I wish I knew what that was.

One moment everything is going well, the next, I'm messing up in a thousand different ways.

The door opens, and Emerson walks in wrapped in an oversized sweatshirt and leggings, her black hair tied back.

She doesn't say a word as she walks to the couch, grabbing my beer and setting it on the table before sitting next to me.

"Dad's still there," she says. Her hands are in her lap, her face twisting painfully like she's moments away from breaking again, and I can't handle it anymore.

Emerson doesn't cry like this—she never has.

I put my arm around her, pulling her in until her arms wrap around my torso. It's like I can feel her tearing apart at the seams.

I lean my cheek against her hair, tightening my grip on her and taking whatever comfort I can get. I hope she's taking the same from me.

With Dad at the hospital, we only have each other.

And Georgia, if you wouldn't have sent her away.

"It's been three days," I say. My voice sounds hollow—empty. "I don't want to lose her, Nemo."

Emerson's grip tightens on me, and it reminds me of when we were younger. Some of the neighbor kids told her that goblins existed, and for weeks, she would come into my room, begging to sleep at the foot of my bed. I was eight, and I used to roll my eyes every time she did it.

I'm glad she did, though.

I'm glad she's here.

"Me neither," she whispers. "I don't want to lose her either."

We sit in the silence, the stillness of the night surrounding us, until Emerson's body begins to shake. She's cried more in the past few days than she did the day she broke her arm.

There are no words of encouragement—nothing I can say that would be true, so I just let her sob until she's done, wiping her face and detaching herself from me.

"You're not allowed to tell me I'm an ugly crier this time, Sawyer." A small smile breaks through as she wipes her eyes again with her sleeve.

I try to force a laugh, the corner of my mouth turning up. "I couldn't if I wanted to."

"Because you're an ugly crier, too?" she asks as her smile widens.

"Shut up." I shove her away from me gently, thankful for the little bit of normalcy this conversation brings.

When her smile fades, her features soften, and I'm not sure I want to hear what she has to say next.

"Have you talked to Georgia?"

My entire body stiffens, the tension running through my shoulders as Emerson looks at me—waiting for an answer.

Guilt slashes through me.

Please don't come over.

I didn't want her to see me struggling, and after what happened at the hospital, I didn't want to hear her talk either. The first day I had held onto the anger, but it slowly left me, replaced with sorrow and something like longing.

It's not that I don't want her here. It's just that—

I don't really know. I'm having a hard enough time piecing together how I feel as it is and knowing Georgia is so closely tied to the source of all this heartache has me feeling—confused.

She *defended* him.

I can't face the guilt of knowing that a decent human would forgive him. He *is* just a kid, but I'm not ready yet.

If I'm being honest, I *want* her here.

"I've sent her a few text messages," I finally answer.

Emerson clears her throat. "I know you don't want to hear this, but she's hurting, too."

I grimace, unable to respond to that.

"Maybe not as much as us—or maybe she is, I'm not sure. Georgia feels things deeply. Though she sometimes likes to keep that to herself."

I nod, letting Emerson continue.

"Sawyer, I don't know what happened in the hospital. I'm sure she said something stupid, but I'm also sure that you probably did, too."

When I look up, Emerson's eyes are glassy again, and the image pulls at every emotion swarming inside of me. There's sorrow and longing, regret and despair. It's quite the cocktail.

"You can't expect perfection in a situation like this." Emerson grabs my hand, squeezing it. "I wish you could, but—" She clears her throat. "You can't expect everyone around you to do exactly the right thing while you break apart." Emerson looks away briefly. "I really think you should talk to her. She wants to be there for you, but only if you want her."

I exhale, leaning my head back against the back of the couch as she lets go of my hand. "Yeah."

"I'm serious," she says. "You're like this. You isolate. I watched you do it when your stupid hamster died. I just don't know if it's the best time to do that. Grief makes us all a little messed up, and you were already kind of messed up to begin with."

My eyes flick to hers, taking in the upward curve at the corner of her mouth. It's contagious, and I allow myself to breathe for a moment.

I told Georgia to leave—I yelled at her. Nobody is immune when it comes to grief, and I'm not sure if she even wants me around.

I keep thinking of the hollowness beneath her own eyes, the way she tried to hold it together—for me.

"Thanks for the speech, Nemo." I say, hiding any real appreciation that lies just beneath the surface.

"Anytime." Emerson stands up, kicking my shin gently. "Come over tomorrow and talk to her. Spend time with both of us. It'll be easier if we have each other."

I nod, not really knowing what I'm going to say to her—hoping that between now and tomorrow night, I'll have it figured out.

THIRTY-SIX

Georgia

I decided to stay after school to gather all my graded samples for my final project.

My mind has been nothing but data, outcomes, learning goals, and assessments. Somehow it was easier to lose myself in the work—easier than letting my own thoughts wander.

I didn't hear from Sawyer today, but I need to just accept that I'm not what he needs, and that's okay.

It has to be okay.

I shove my key into the deadbolt, turning it and jiggling the handle until the door opens.

As soon as it does, my stomach feels like lead when the familiar voices meet me. I drop my schoolbag on the couch and move toward the galley kitchen where the light is on.

Emerson sits against the cabinets on the floor, biting

her nail.

It's when I look up to see Sawyer at the stove that my body goes stock still. His gray t-shirt clings to his back, black sweatpants hanging from his hips as he flips something over in the heated pan.

"Hey," Emerson says, standing up to drag me into a hug. "You're not allowed to pull away," she says into my hair. "I'm the sad one, so you have to give me this hug." She squeezes me tighter. "Besides," she starts. "You're sad, too."

I let out a strained laugh and wrap my arms around her. I don't want to admit that I need it—we all need it.

When Emerson breaks away, I see Sawyer turned around, spatula in one hand as his other clutches the granite countertop. Dark circles are carved beneath his eyes, his skin pale, and the corner of his mouth turned down.

"I didn't mean to interrupt," I say. I'm tugging on my shirt, wringing my hands together—anything to ease whatever emotion is bubbling up inside of me.

After everything that happened—he just shut me out. I could be angry at him for it, but what's the use?

"It's not like I didn't know you'd be here, Georgia." A wan smile tugs at Sawyer's lips. "This is your house."

"Right."

Emerson looks between us, and the air feels stale—stagnant—like a storm is waiting to roll in.

She clears her throat. "I'm going to step out for a second."

And just like that, she's gone, leaving me to stand in front of her brother, feeling two feet tall. I can't help but believe I may deserve that feeling.

"I made crepes," he says, breaking the silence. "For all of us. I think they're a pretty good copy of what we had on our trip."

I nod, the words on the tip of my tongue. I'm too afraid to speak, but. As Sawyer turns off the stove and stares at me, I muster up the courage despite the twisting and churning of my stomach.

"I'm so—"

I don't get to finish. His arms are around me, lemongrass and pancake batter invading my lungs. My head is against his chest, and I exhale for what feels like the first time in days.

"Just don't say anything," he whispers. "I've been selfish."

I can't help the small laugh that escapes. "Okay." My chest is burning as the silence continues stretching between us.

I tighten my arms around his torso, holding him steady when I feel moisture. Pulling away, I look up, noticing the heavy tears gathered in Sawyer's brown eyes. Everything in me cracks and breaks as I bring my fingers up to brush them away.

He closes his eyes, his hand wrapping around my wrist when he leans into the touch. I can't help the way my own tears flow down, silently streaming. They aren't for me though—they're for him.

He's breaking.

"I'm glad to see you," he whispers. "I didn't think I would be, but I am."

A smile tugs at my lips. "I thought maybe you were

tired of me after ten days in Paris."

"I thought so, too."

He drags my hand from his cheek, his fingers warm around my wrist as he places a kiss on my palm.

Sawyer's eyes meet mine. "I'm sorry I pushed you away," he says. "After everything that's happened—" Sawyer clears his throat. "I need you, Georgia. Here. With me."

All the memories and feelings from our trip rush back to me, spilling out in the way I trail my fingers over his bottom lip. "Emerson may kill us if we don't eat soon."

Sawyer chuckles, and the sound loosens something inside of me. "Right," he says. "Then we better eat."

~

"Do you remember when she started crying at that stupid cartoon short?" Sawyer says as we sit on the floor by the couches. He's holding a beer in one hand, my fingers laced through the other.

Emerson's brow furrows. "No?" she says.

"It was when you were really little, Nemo. You got so panicked you started insisting that she eat the quesadilla you had for lunch. You shoved it in her mouth, thinking it would make her feel better, and she just laughed." The smile splitting Sawyer's face warms something in me. "You've always been abusive."

"Oh, like the time you became obsessed with April Fools' pranks and poked a hole in your soda, having me drink it right before Aunt Riley's wedding." Emerson is laughing now. "That's abuse, Sawyer. Mom was so mad because you ruined my dress."

"Should have been smarter," he says, bringing the beer to his lips and taking a drink. "And Aunt Riley shouldn't have made the flower girl wear white, too."

We've been sitting on the floor for hours, talking about Sandra. I've mostly listened to Emerson and Sawyer telling stories with Sawyer's hand in mine, squeezing gently every once in a while, but there are stories I've been able to tell. The more we talk, the lighter the weight—though it's still there.

"I should probably go to bed," Emerson says, pushing against the couch to stand up. "Dad said he's staying at the hospital tonight."

Something shifts in Sawyer's expression, and I lean my head against his shoulder, refusing to let him go.

"Right," he whispers as Emerson exits the living room.

It's late, and the darkness seems to engulf the entire apartment, swallowing the dim light from the lamp on our end table.

"I should go," Sawyer says, but he doesn't move.

"Or not." I remove my head from his shoulder, turning up to look at his face. He's exhausted and tired—hollow. "Where are you planning to go?" I ask.

"Home."

My eyes are flicking between his, trying to read how he's feeling despite knowing I will never fully understand.

I lick my lip, my heart thrashing in my chest as I say the next words. "Please don't be alone, Sawyer."

Tears are welling in his eyes again. The image

breaking my heart so thoroughly, I can't help but wish I could take his pain—leech it from his body and walk through his hurt myself.

Sawyer nods, and my rapid heartbeat settles.

"Stay with me," I whisper into the darkness, hoping like hell that he will accept my offer. "Please," my voice is barely audible now. "Just stay."

Sawyer leans his forehead on mine, his hand rising to my face as his thumb strokes my cheek. "Okay."

When we get back to my room, Sawyer doesn't hesitate to crawl into the bed with me. He rests his head on my stomach, his arm wrapped around me like I'm some kind of lifeline.

I stare at the ceiling, watching the fan spin and running my fingers through the hair near the base of his neck, feeling the tears stain my shirt.

I'm trying not to cry too, but it's useless, so I let myself break with him. It's the only thing I can think to do.

It's not like I haven't been carrying my own hurt, and I think he realizes that. I know he does.

"I'm glad you're here, Georgia," he whispers, and my chest swells with emotion, warm, but heavy, like the pressure of his head on my stomach, his body curled up next to mine.

"I'm glad you're here, too."

That feeling blooms, and the thought comes to my mind, loud and insistent.

I love you.

I don't dare say it out loud—not now—not this soon, but I know.

I just know.

And something about the way Sawyer's arm tightens around me, the way his breathing steadies as the night stretches on outside the windows of my room, makes me start to believe that maybe he knows it, too.

THIRTY-SEVEN

Sawyer

Something wakes me up in the middle of the night, my limbs still tangled with Georgia's.

Her heartbeat is slow and steady as it pounds in my ears, my head still on her stomach, arms wrapped around her waist.

I listen to her breathe, and my mind settles, my worries easing in her presence.

I don't want to leave this spot.

I want to stay suspended in this place until the nightmare is over—until I know the horrors have disappeared.

Georgia stirs when a knock sounds at the door, and I lift my head. Leaning down to kiss her before getting up and answering.

Emerson stands on the other side, her eyes wide with hope. "Dad called," she says. "She's awake—stable."

My whole body feels like it's been submerged in relief as I stare at my sister. She's already wearing her shoes, and her hand squeezes her phone.

Georgia comes up behind me, warm fingers wrapping around my arm. "Do you want me to stay here?" she asks.

I look down at her, and her expression tells me she would do anything I asked.

Whatever you need.

I know she meant it.

And I was the asshole that didn't recognize all the ways she was hurting herself.

I pushed her away, and I don't plan to make that same mistake again.

Shaking my head, I wrap my arm around her shoulders, pulling her closer as the hope rises in my chest.

"No," I say. "I want you there."

And I do—

I can't think of anyone I want more.

~

My dad stands in the lobby with the doctor as Emerson bursts forward to wrap her arms around him.

He looks tired.

I can't let go of Georgia's hand—not for anything. Regardless of what happened before, in the end, she was there. I don't want her to leave again. I didn't want her to leave before, but I just didn't know that, yet.

Emerson was right when she told me I push people

away.

"You're all very lucky," the doctor says. "These outcomes are not—common." He's holding his hands in front of him, brows furrowed as he looks between us. "Most patients waking up from a medically induced coma will have complications. So far, we aren't finding any, but we will need to continue to monitor."

"Can we see her?" Emerson jumps in, and I'm not sure the doctor could say no if he wanted to—not with the way my sister's eyes light up with hope.

"Yes, however, we ask that visitation is restricted to family, only."

I nod, feeling Georgia's gaze slide in my direction. I don't look at her, just tug her hand closer and nod. "We all are." I clear my throat. "Family, that is."

The doctor nods before leading us back. He doesn't bother to question us—taking our word for it, and I'm thankful for that because I still can't pull my hand away from Georgia's.

"Are you sure I should come back here?" Georgia is whispering as we trail behind my dad and sister.

"What do you mean?" I question, and she raises her brows.

"Family."

"You've been to our Thanksgiving," I say, a smile stretching across my face. "You're family."

I finally let go of her hand, wrapping my arm around her and pulling her closer. My lips press against her temple as we make our way to the room where my mom is sitting up, medical equipment surrounding her.

Her eyes are swollen—but they're open.

My heart cracks, and relief washes over me.

When I turn to Georgia, I don't see anything aside from one word that echoes over and over in my mind, but I don't dare say it.

I just let the feeling take me under as I turn to my mother—thankful.

EPILOGUE

One Year Later

Sawyer

"Do you think your mom is going to like it?"

"Georgia, you've asked me that same question at least fifty times. It's an apron with a giant pug on it. Of course she will like it."

Georgia pulls the apron from the bag again, inspecting it as we walk through the mall together.

My family is planning on having dinner at the restaurant tomorrow with Georgia's parents, who are flying in tonight. I've met Jason and Barb a few times, and Georgia calls them frequently—even more now that she's taken a teaching job in Michigan instead of back where they live in Portland.

"We should get something for my parents, too," she says, threading her fingers through mine. "And maybe your dad."

I roll my eyes. "Yes. Christmas in May. What a fantastic idea."

She leans into me, irritated by my mocking remark. "What do you have to complain about?" she says. "You own a successful restaurant. You're practically made of money."

"That's not true." I can't fight the way my chest lights up when she talks like this—a reminder of how we started.

I never want it to end.

Georgia stops, cocking her eyebrow when I face her and place my hands on her waist to pull her in.

She pretends to be immune, but I notice the way her eyes flick to my lips briefly—the subtle change in breathing that has my head spinning.

I lean down to kiss her before speaking again. "You're the rich one. I didn't know high school teachers made six figures."

"Ha. Ha. Very funny."

She's smiling, and I catch sight of the photobooth standing against the wall behind her, thinking it's the perfect time to tell her.

I drag her to the booth as she scoffs and mutters protests, though I'm not fooled. She's a sap, and I know she's going to be obsessed with whatever pictures we take. I'm certain they will be on our fridge in no time.

Georgia halts just before I can part the curtain, and I look back at her. "Humor me," I say.

Without putting up a fight, she lets me drag her onto the small bench. I'm fiddling away with the buttons and trying to find where to dispose of the quarters weighing down my wallet.

That's when I see the card reader.

No quarters, then.

I grab my debit card, swiping it a few times before it finally takes, and now I'm racing against the clock.

"So, I think I'm going to have the new head chef take over the restaurant for a few weeks once the school year ends."

"Why?" Georgia turns to me, ignoring the countdown happening on the screen as her brow furrows.

I have ten seconds to capture this.

I pull out my phone, quickly tapping on the app that displays our flights. I turn the screen to face her and wait for the realization.

5.

4.

3.

"We're going to Paris."

She gasps. "We are not!" The first photo snaps as the timer resets. I can't help but sneak a glance toward the screen, noticing the smile on my face, and the shocked expression on hers—the one where her brows are lowered, and her mouth is hanging open like a fish.

She's going to hate that photo.

Good.

"I said we are going to Paris. Again. I have the whole thing worked out. We are taking a trip with all my *fancy money.*"

That's when the smile splits her face, splitting my chest right along with it. Her eyes light, blazing green with excitement.

The shutter goes off.

That's a good one.

Fuck. I love her.

"Are we going to another wedding?" she asks as the countdown resets.

I release a laugh, bringing my hand up to her cheek and feeling her soft skin there. I skim my thumb along her lower lip, my ego swelling as her lips part. "No. Just us going on a trip for fun."

She's staring at me now, and my heart rate picks up, the smile dropping from my own mouth, my body humming with desire.

She's so fucking beautiful.

Especially when she's this happy.

"Sawyer." Her voice is a low whisper as tension crackles in the small booth, encasing us in electricity and warmth.

The shutter sounds again.

That one is practically porn.

Oops.

Georgia stands up and shuffles awkwardly in the small space, and I breathe out a laugh.

She's straddling me, looking down at me like I've captured the moon and the stars and hung them specifically for her. It's nothing like that, but I'm pretty sure if she asked, I would try to make it happen.

I can be very determined.

I turn to the side a bit, resting my hands on her waist as we share breath.

Her lips are on mine, and I'm vaguely aware of another photo. If I remember correctly, there should be more, but all thoughts exit my mind as she scoots forward, grinding against me and deepening the kiss.

Yeah, this is definitely porn.

I hope there aren't kids watching the monitor outside.

I can't bring myself to stop.

Georgia's hands are in my hair, her mouth moving in time with the beating of my heart—the blissful happiness that washes over me in her presence.

She breaks the kiss, resting her forehead on mine. "Thank you," she whispers. "This is the best gift ever."

I smile, highly doubting she will agree with the declaration for long. I have a feeling that the gift she'll receive when we get there—after food and a long nap, of course— will top this one by a *lot*.

At least, I hope it will.

That part still makes me a little nervous since I don't have it all completely planned out. I have the ring. I have her parents coming for dinner tomorrow, but I have no idea where I'm going to do it—no idea if she'll even say yes.

Emerson is going to murder me when she finds out I didn't tell her, but the girl can't keep a secret—not from Georgia.

Mom's the only one that knows.

"I think it's going to be fun," I say before she leans in again, dragging her fingers through my hair and tugging until I'm utterly at her mercy.

Fucking hell.

I don't care to stop, but then the worry creeps in—the worry that some middle school boys are currently having their sexual awakening.

We might get arrested for public indecency.

Can't have that.

I break the kiss. "We need to go home." My breathing is labored, and I'm trying like hell not to think about the way her body is pressing down on my—

Shit.

She grinds her hips forward, leaning down to kiss my neck. "Why?" she asks. "You don't like this."

"I like it too much." My voice is raspy. "That's why we need to go home."

"Fine," she says, removing herself from my lap.

When we get out of the photobooth, she grabs the pictures, and I'm certain the last one is not safe for work—not at all.

"I think when we get to France, I should start my animal collection," she starts, wrapping her arms around my torso as we walk. The bag with my mom's apron draped over her arm. "I might get something like a fox."

"That's what you're choosing?" I question.

"That's what I'm choosing *first.*" She's smiling now, her eyes lighting up. "Then I might get a bear. Maybe an owl." She lets go, tilting her head and stopping in the middle of the marble floors. "It's going to be very expensive. You better start making more meals."

"Yeah, yeah," I say, dragging her back to me and kissing her temple. "You've been using me for my money since the very beginning."

"Technically, Sadie's money. Which reminds me, are they still coming in August?"

Sadie and Warren weren't upset when we finally admitted the truth about how our relationship started, and I'm thankful that Warren found time to take a trip here to hang out with us.

I think the only reason they forgave us was because, by that time, we were actually together.

"They are, why?"

"I'm just excited, is all."

I look down at her, our steps synced as we move toward the exit. "More excited than you are for France?"

"Oh, absolutely not."

"Good, because I may have left out one small detail." I know she suspects a joking remark—I just can't help myself. "I'm actually paying for the trip with photos of your feet you sold online."

Georgia laughs as we slip out into the warm Spring air, a breeze weaving through the parking lot and ruffling her hair.

"Do you need more for your private collection?" she asks, cocking an eyebrow.

"That's disgusting." My nose scrunches up, and I see our car. "No feet needed, but we are definitely going to the bed when we get home."

She grabs my hand, squeezing it before pulling me to the car. "If we even make it that far."

I smile. "Sounds like a grand adventure."

Acknowledgments

I hate this part of the book about as much as Georgia hated Sawyer.

It gives me anxiety to think I may forget someone, so let's start with this—

Thank you, world?

That should cover it.

I want to thank my amazing editor, Kenna. I say this in every single book, but I would be lost without you. I would be drowning in comma splices, too many *anyways*, and all the wrong imagery. You save my books and deserve the world for it.

I want to thank Reanna for proofing and catching all of the things I miss. You have incredible eyesight, and I honestly don't understand how you do it. Thank you for all of your encouragement, and of course, for existing. I would have way worse imposter syndrome if it weren't for you.

I want to say a big old thank you to my husband for letting me write. Thank you for taking care of our kid when I enter the editing rabbit hole. Thank you for being the original hot boyfriend to inspire the book boyfriends I write. Also, I just love you.

I want to say thank you to Wednesday for alpha reading this book while it was still a mess. You're the real deal, and I'm eternally grateful for you.

I want to thank Barbara for reading this before it was fully edited and gassing me up. I want to be you when I grow up.

Thank you, Ali, for narrating another book for me,

and more importantly, thank you for your friendship.

A huge thank you to Lisa King for being my supervising teacher during my student teaching placement. I have heard so many horror stories, and I can honestly say, you helped me fall in love with teaching and grow in confidence. Thank you for adopting my family during that time, taking days off so I could get sub money when we were stuck eating ramen, and for being exactly who you are. I wanted to honor you with a character in this book, so . . . here you go!

I have to thank Becca for inspiring this book. I know you are not a big fan of romantic comedies, but I'm glad you enjoyed this one. Honestly, I was so nervous.

Thank you to Sawyer Owens for being my favorite book boyfriend I have ever written. I am drooling.

Finally, thank you, dear reader, for keeping my writing journey alive. I would literally be unemployed without you.

About the Author

Emmie J. Holland is the pen name used by Emma Steinbrecher for her romance books. Emma Steinbrecher typically writes New Adult Fantasy and New Adult Romantic Comedy.

She lives in Ohio with her two dogs, her son, and her husband.

When she is not writing, she enjoys hiking, learning new hobbies, and reading.

If you're anxious to read any of her other works, here is a list of the books.

A Clan of Wolves Duology

A Clan of Wolves by Emma Steinbrecher (Book 1)
A House of Witches by Emma Steinbrecher (Book 2)

The Death Hunting Trilogy

The Death Hunting by Emma Steinbrecher (Book 1)
The Raidan Awakening by Emma Steinbrecher (Book 2)
The Light Conquering (Book 3) releases July 2023

Emmie J. Holland

The Unbelievable Misadventures of Olive Finch by Emmie J. Holland

AUTHOR WEBSITE

Don't forget to check out Emmie's website for signed books, exclusive content, and a newsletter that is literally so inconsistent, it won't bother you at all. You can, however, get first dibs on ARC sign-ups and other announcements through the newsletter, so it *is* worth something.

CPSIA information can be obtained
at www.ICGtesting.com
Printed in the USA
BVHW032316130223
658422BV00004B/65